OF UNKNOWN ORIGIN

MOVIE TIE-IN EDITION

CHAUNCEY G. PARKER III

For my Family

Movie Tie-In Edition

Originally published as The Visitor.

Copyright © 1981 Chauncey G. Parker III.

All Rights Reserved. The characters and events in this book are fictitious. Any similarity to real persons, living, dead or undead is coincidental and not intended by the author.

No part of this book may be reproduced in any form or by any electronic or mechanical means, including information storage and retrieval systems, without permission in writing from the publisher, except by a reviewer who may quote brief passages in a review.

Encyclopocalypse Publications
www.encyclopocalypse.com

Acknowledgments

Grateful thanks, first and foremost, to Victor A. Mahoney, a teacher of the first rank who shared his learning, his time and his good sense so unsparingly; to my agents Molly Friedrich and Aaron Priest, who were the first to believe and never quit, more than once being called upon to turn tears of despair into laughter and hope; to Nicholas LeR. King, who read and corrected my original manuscript and, despite the experience, urged me to persevere; to Thomas L. Pulling, who somehow could always sense when the moments were darkest and unfailingly brought light to them; to my editors Joan Sanger and Bette Alexander, who pointed out the weaknesses, showed me how to paper them over, and have made me appear smarter than I am; to Allerton Cushman, whose belief in me, though often tested, never faltered; to Philip L. Geyelin, who helped me turn a pivotal comer and onto the right course at last; to Lorraine Rodano, who coped with my handwriting in the days before I had learned to type, so to speak; to Dr. John Roberts, Jack Flood, John Koch and Tom Farrell, whose technical expertise did much to keep me honest; to the Rotary Club of Kingston which so generously bent its rules to accommodate my writing schedule; to the Shaeffer Eaton Division of Textron, Inc., the makers of erasable typewriter paper; to the copier industry one and all; and last but not least, as they say, to the New York City rat whose story this might have been.

C. G. P. III
Kingston, New York

PART ONE

One

IT WAS MONDAY NIGHT, one of those especially sultry evenings in Manhattan more common to mid-August than to early July. Bartlett Hughes was sitting in his kitchen near the fully open Dutch door that led to the garden, alternately dipping into a stack of mail and the cup of vichyssoise which he had poured from a can he had found in the refrigerator. He had returned to his town house an hour or so earlier, having spent the extended Fourth of July weekend with his wife, Meg, and their three children at the southern tip of Maine. This was their fifth summer there and, as always, the house felt empty without them.

Nevertheless, Bart had to admit that he relished his summers in New York in spite of the occasional loneliness and the often suffocating heat. It was his chance to have the house he loved so much to himself.

From the outside it appeared to be just one more run-of-the-mill Upper Eastside brownstone identifiable by its reddish color and dual entrances, one at the top of a steep stoop, the other behind a grilled door beneath it. Its nondescript appearance was quite intentional for Bart had no wish to excite the curiosity of either night prowler or tax assessor unnecessarily.

But on the inside, it was a different matter. Bart and Meg, in conjunction with the renovating architect, had overlooked no detail in restoring a rundown rooming house into the gracious home it had once been. The renovation had taken all of four months and the house had become a true reflection of their combined personalities as well as the great love and effort each had put into it.

The ceilings were high, bordered by carved moldings with an ornate rosette at the center of each. Most of the rooms had fireplaces with handsome mantles of marble or wood. On the second floor at the front of the house was a library which doubled as the guest room. Its walls were lined with built-in bookshelves filled to capacity with the leather-bound collections Bart had inherited from his grandfather. A majestic crystal chandelier hung in the vestibule, Oriental rugs covered the polished oak floors, and English regency furniture graced every room in the house.

Bart and Meg's bedroom was on the third floor overlooking the garden. Little Bart was down the hall and the girls were on the fourth floor, each in her own room separated by a bathroom.

The kitchen was a generous, cheerful place painted a bright yellow. Matching yellow formica covered the tops of all the counters and the table where the family had breakfast. A handsome Victorian love seat dug out of an attic by some relative provided a cozy touch.

Adjacent to the gleaming, modern kitchen stretched a garden, fifty feet deep, tended with loving care by Meg, and thoroughly enjoyed by Bart and the children. The large magnolia tree at its far end exploded into thick flower mid-April each year, signaling that the cold and the snow and the slush were gone for good.

Bart had been raised in a house himself, and one of his prime concerns in considering New York for his career had been the certain condemnation to years of apartment living. He detested the lack of privacy, the forced conviviality at the elevators and the communal garbage facilities. And so, not surprisingly, he had leaped at the first house to come along his family liked and he could afford.

To a person, their former neighbors had crowed a patronizing "You'll be back!", but it had been Bart and Meg who had enjoyed the last laugh. The house had proved an unrivaled success, and they both knew they had found the one way to live in the city which would be entirely to their liking.

As Bart glanced around the kitchen with pride, his attention was suddenly diverted by a swiftly moving streak of grayish brown darting from beneath his chair. "Oh, goddammit to hell! Not again!" he exclaimed with a mixture of alarm and disgust as he slapped the latest copy of *Newsweek* onto the table. He thought he had spotted the stiff, pointed tail but he could not be sure, it had happened so fast. But the chances were better than even that it had been another mouse which had bolted into the kitchen from the garden.

Bart's eyes remained riveted to the spot where he thought he had seen it disappear under the clothes washer at the far end of the room.

Slowly, silently, he leaned forward toward the table and rested his forearms there. Spontaneously his gaze narrowed, to increase its sharpness. His breathing grew shallow, his pulse beat quickened.

Time was of the utmost.

As long as the mouse remained unfamiliar with its new

surroundings, a certain, limited, tactical superiority would rest with Bart. However, this delicate balance was sure to change and the conflict be forced to run its entire, dreary course. Bart had learned this lesson the hard way and he was not about to disregard it now.

In what seemed a single bound, he was at the washing machine, had dropped to his knees and was peering anxiously underneath.

The blackness made it impossible to be sure, but Bart was virtually certain the mouse was there. It was huddled about two feet in and looked to be panting.

Of course, it could be his imagination, up to its old tricks. Bart realized that. But he was unwilling to leave anything to chance, even so.

He needed something long and narrow to reach the mouse. It crossed his mind to go after the flashlight, too, but since he could see his adversary, there was really no need. He raced to the broom closet instead.

A slightly damp mop was tucked into a far corner. It must have been there some time. The acrid smell of mildew it threw off caught him in the throat. He hacked involuntarily, but decided to use it nonetheless.

Doing his best to avoid breathing through his nose, he grabbed the mop by its head and fell once again to his knees in front of the clothes washer.

"Come to Papa!" he said confidently, shoving the wooden handle purposefully under the machine and starting to swing it back and forth in large, sweeping motions. Momentarily, he expected to establish some sort of contact, causing the mouse to burst into the open, in search of new sanctuary.

The prospect bothered him somewhat, for he had never had to kill a mouse on the run before, and all too easily conjured up repugnant visions of it splattering every which way when he did. But this by no means diluted his resolve to get the job done. Resolutely, he pressed on, poking here, prodding there into distant comers.

It was taking longer than he felt it should, and he was fast growing dispirited and irritable. The dress shirt he was wearing was clutching at his armpits and clinging to his back. He yearned to rip it off.

The sum total of his efforts thus far consisted only of dislodging a half dozen hard gray dust balls, a few shards of linoleum, and a miscellany of other evidence that no vacuum cleaner had passed through in a long while.

"Son of a bitch!" he spat out, feeling himself being dragged inexorably into another prolonged conflict.

He could no longer delay getting the flashlight and hurried off in search of it. It was in none of the usual places and his impatience to find it made its pursuit seem endless. About to abandon the effort, he chanced to spot something metallic and shiny, under his son's bed, on the fourth floor.

"*Damn* that kid!" he muttered, racing with it back to the field of battle.

On the way, he speculated what the mouse would do when, bathed in light, it realized it was through and there was no chance of escape. Stand firm, bracing for the inevitable? Panic? Chance one last desperate spurt for freedom, despite the odds?

Suppose it had taken advantage of his absence to move to a new location. What then? He would worry about that when he had to.

Eager to get it over with, Bart knelt once more before the clothes washer and clicked on the flashlight. Its batteries were weak, the beam timorous and blinking. But it was better than nothing. The orange glow spilled into where the mop handle could not reach, sparing little, showing no mercy.

Suddenly, he saw it, not the mouse exactly, but its round, stationary shadow, cast against the base of the back wall. Bart's body tensed. He estimated there was just enough clearance for the mop handle, and stealthily began to inch its tip toward his objective at a point between the wall and the crouching mouse. Progress was agonizingly slow, but he made no attempt to speed it, mindful that the least disturbance would break the hypnotic effect of the flashlight's beam, provoking the mouse into taking flight. Finally, he had his probe where he wanted it. Taking a slow deep breath, he gripped the handle tightly and, with a mighty roar, jerked it full force toward him. The instant the mop handle cleared the outer edge of the washer, Bart raised it high over his head and brought it crashing down onto his target. It made a thunderous clap. His eyes blinked reflexively. A deathlike stillness fell over the empty house.

Bart slumped back onto his haunches and closed his eyes. Gradually, the tightness throughout his entire body began to subside. His throat and mouth were dry as parchment and his head throbbed brutally. But it was over. Thank God.

Deliberately he avoided looking at what he had done. It could not be a pretty sight, and he had little appetite for it. Instead, he immediately went for something with which to clean up the mess, quickly coming across an old dustpan in the cleaning cupboard. It would do nicely.

Still diverting his gaze, Bart stooped down and prepared to scoop up the battered carcass. The mop handle lay as he had dropped it. And underneath, flattened almost beyond recognition, were the earthly remains of a hard gray dust ball.

It had been not quite a year since his long ordeal with the mice had ended. That affair had also started innocently enough with the discovery of a solitary mouse. Bart had seen no reason to become unduly concerned and, as a result, before he had awakened to the true extent of the problem, it had blossomed into epidemic proportions.

When Bart had moved into the neighborhood, it was in a state of total upheaval. Many of those who had come from the old country to forge new lives, forty or fifty years earlier, were steadily dying off. Their children were themselves moving away in pursuit of better schools and a less harried way of life in the suburbs. Everywhere, the handiwork of real estate developers was in evidence, from the skeletal remains of buildings being renovated to the vacant lots where others once had stood.

While the human element may have been the most visible, there were others equally affected by the changing times. Immense colonies of mice, ants, cockroaches, spiders, roving alley cats, marauding termites—these, too, were being uprooted, driven into the streets in droves, seeking alternative sources of food, new lodgings, a fresh start.

Bart should have foreseen that his house would stand as a beacon in the night. But he hadn't. And this, of course, had led directly to that horde of mice making his home theirs.

Unquestionably, the most ominous aspect of this dreadful business had been its effect on Bart's mental state. Before long, he had become utterly obsessed. What the mice could not achieve through procreation, Bart supplemented by his active imagination. He suspected them literally everywhere in the house. To this day, a year after the fact, he had to make himself guard against automatically attributing any and all strange noises, day or night, to another scurrying mouse on the prowl.

And then, there were the recurring nightmares. They, too, helped keep the memory alive, like the one in which he wildly sought to beat off wave upon wave of mice swarming over the foot of his bed before they could reach his face and smother him. This was the most frequent, but there were others, all vivid, all frightful, all alarmingly real.

The plague had lasted in excess of three months, and by its end had Bart truly fearing for his sanity. It was unthinkable that anything like it could be unfolding anew.

Bart stared disconsolately at the crushed dust ball for a moment and then resumed the search with the flashlight, up, down, sideways, but to no avail. Real or imagined, the mouse was gone. Vanished.

He did not return the mop to the cleaning closet, preferring to leave it to air and dry on the landing of the stairwell leading to the playroom in the basement. As he closed the door and reentered the kitchen, the telephone rang. It was his wife, Meg.

"Hi, there!" she greeted him cheerily.

"Hi, there, yourself, sweetheart!" he tried to respond in kind, wanting to sound casual, on top of things.

"Just calling to make sure you got home okay. You sound all out of breath."

"Had to run for the telephone," he said, undecided whether or not to go into the real reason.

"Oh!" Meg breathed, reassured. "What's it like down there?"

"Hotter'n hell. Feels like rain. Much rather be up there with you, I'll tell you that. It was a great weekend."

"I loved it, too. Went by too fast, though. They always do...and I just hate thinking about your not coming up again for two weeks. I've already started ticking off the hours," she said with a light laugh.

"Same here," he said, preoccupied, deciding to go ahead. "Say! It looks like we may be in for another round with the mice, goddammit!"

"Oh, no! What makes you think that?"

"Well, it's my own stupid fault, but I think I saw it barrel in from the garden...right under my chair. It's so goddam hot and airless tonight, I forgot, I guess. Left the bottom of the door open, too."

"Oh, Bart," she said, wanting to appear understanding, but a touch of reproof came through, nonetheless.

"Yeah, I know," he agreed, catching it. "But then, the damn thing vanished."

"Maybe it ran back into the garden," Meg suggested, trying to be helpful.

"I hadn't thought of that. But maybe. Or maybe, I just imagined the whole thing," he said weakly, looking for a denial.

"Oh, I doubt that, Bart," Meg obliged. "More likely the garden."

"You know, you may be right at that. It could've decided this was no place to make a home." He was trying to persuade himself as much as talking for Meg's benefit. "Jesus, I hope so!"

"Makes sense to me." Her tone was comforting.

Meg's telephone call had been reassuring, and Bart was grateful to her for it. She knew how to get through the clutter, to the heart of the matter, to see things unemotionally, in their true light.

What Meg had said about the mouse fleeing back into the garden *did* make sense. Or in any event, it was as solid a theory as any to account for its disappearance into thin air, so mystifyingly, so suddenly, so absolutely. And yet...

He decided to have another look under the washer and dryer in case he had missed something, some telltale clue that the mouse had been there, that he had not been fantasizing. With the pressure off, he could take his time and did.

Meticulously he explored the area with the flashlight. Twice the weak, orange beam cast a solid, round shadow against the base of the back wall. He knew better this time than to think it anything but what it was. He pulled the vacuum cleaner from the broom closet. Its whirring bounced off the bare kitchen walls, insistent, abrasive. A miscellany of flotsam and jetsam clickety-clicked into its long, metal throat.

Bart climbed on top of the machines, beamed the light down the back wall, through a maze of feeder and drain hoses. He shone the light behind the floor cabinets, into every crevice, nook and cranny, wherever it would extend.

If ever there had been a mouse, all traces of it were gone from there now, of that much Bart was certain.

Good old Meg, he thought affectionately, turning off the lights and heading for bed. She had sized up the situation perfectly.

Two

BART SLEPT FITFULLY. Apprehensively, would perhaps be a more fitting description. Try as he would to prevent them, thoughts of the mouse kept intruding, eating at him, waking him. At times, he vividly recalled its terrified expression, beady black eyes, nervously twitching nose and whiskers. Yet, at others, he was assailed by doubt, just as certain he had seen nothing more than a hard, gray dust ball, and that his imagination had filled in the rest.

Throughout the night, he had kept listening for some signal, but there had been none. And in the morning, he was able to head for the office cheered and optimistic, prepared to put the whole episode behind him.

It had been just twelve years since Bart had started with the bank, fresh from graduate school, a master's degree under one arm and a briefcase bulging with hope and promise under the other. He had worked hard, played the game, cultivated the right people in the right places, sidestepped the pitfalls and suffered no real setbacks. His reward had been a steadily improving corporate and financial respectability.

An assistant vice-president with five people reporting

to him, he could reasonably look forward to a full vicepresidency in the not too distant future and, if all went well, to more beyond that. He had as much as been told this by Eliot Riverton, the head of the pension-trust department in which he worked.

In addition to overseeing the investment management responsibilities of his unit, Bart was also often called upon to make corporate presentations on behalf of his department, particularly the difficult ones. Sometimes it would be to solicit a new piece of business, but at others, such as the one coming up in three days, it would be to defend a lackluster investment performance and the consequent threat of account withdrawal.

Bart was extremely effective as a public speaker, not only because he was a quick thinker but also because he conveyed at once an impression of sincerity, of truly caring, plus the reassurance of competence. Then too, he was blessed with an imposing physical presence.

Just over six feet, he was generally regarded as a handsome man, standing very erect, almost proud. His well-proportioned frame and trim body gave him the look of an athlete, a tennis player perhaps, and made whatever suit he bought off the rack seem to have been tailor-made. Someone who had known him for many years once said of him, "Whether he's winning or losing, Bart Hughes always looks like a winner."

Up for client review Friday was the department's biggest money earner. It had not fared well during the past year. Coupled with this was the recent promotion of a financial vicepresident, who was suspected of viewing this as presenting an ideal opportunity to pluck this plum for his new empire. No one envied Bart the mission Eliot Riverton had assigned him, and just about everybody, especially Bart himself, saw the connection between his success or failure and his own vicepresidential prospects.

He had scheduled a meeting with his staff for that morning in order to lay out his battle strategy. Shortly before ten-thirty, they began to gather in his office. Bart enjoyed the feeling of action, of dispatching people to right and left, and before very long, he had his scenario for Friday taking shape.

He found the session invigorating and was well pleased with its results. With a little luck, he should be able to ward off the challenge successfully.

But it was all downhill for him after his captive audience had departed on their appointed tasks. The day turned routine, monotonous, and was plagued by empty periods which were quickly filled with thoughts about the mouse.

As the day neared its end, Bart became convinced that Meg's theory must be written off as only so much wishful thinking. Whoever heard of a house mouse voluntarily relinquishing newly found refuge?

In its stead, the possibility that he could have hallucinated the arrival regained its appeal, and this despite what it implied about the general state of his mental health. It was preferable to the remaining alternative that he was standing at the threshold of another period of progressive hostilities, his life about to be thrown into turmoil, his home taken over, his property ravaged.

Bart left the office promptly at five knowing that, fact or fantasy, the doubt surrounding this mouse had to be resolved, one way or another and the sooner the better.

Immediately on arriving home he retrieved the four traps left over from the old days. He laid them out before the clothes washer, neatly spaced in a wide arc. He had his routine down pat Naturally, there were other places he could have put them, but this was where he had last "seen" the mouse. Long and torturous experience had convinced him of the folly of speculation and of the need to work strictly with facts. Besides, chances were, after twenty-four hours without food, the cheddar-cheese bait would be irresistible, no matter where they were.

Satisfied that the traps were as they should be, Bart mixed himself his nightly scotch on the rocks, opened a can of beef stew and put it to simmer on the stove. Then he sat down to enjoy his drink and to watch the evening news on television.

When he turned in for the night, Bart was optimistic that tomorrow he would have his answer. The alternatives, after all, were cut and dry. Either all the traps would be as he had left them, thereby going a long way toward confirming that the mouse had been illusory, or there would be one dead rodent clamped in the pitiless embrace of one of them.

In the circumstances, he should have slept peacefully, but it was not to be. At approximately two-thirty, he was brusquely wakened by what sounded to him like the familiar rustling of a mouse directly overhead. The rug in his daughter Evie's room had been dispatched to the cleaners after a tough winter.

It was difficult to tell, therefore, whether the mouse was scurrying on the bare floor or busily at work under it, in the ceiling of Bart's bedroom. More puzzling still, each time his eyes would pop open and he would try to pinpoint the what and the where, the action would stop, only to resume promptly the instant he would start to drift off again.

Then it happened. Something caused a piece of plaster to break off inside the wall, plummet past his room and down three floors, until it could be heard no more. Bart sat bolt upright in his bed, eyes popping, and listened. He pressed his ear to the cool wall and strained to hear. Nothing. Faint strains of classical music wafted from a lighted apartment across the way. Someone else was having trouble sleeping, he thought, wondering their reason.

But from inside the wall of his bedroom, all continued still. How should he interpret the suddenness of the quiet? Had the stop-and-go scurrying overhead been Bart's darting in and out of dreams? And what about the chunk of falling plaster? Had it simply broken off of its own weight, as sometimes happens in old houses? Or had it been the mouse, which had accidentally stepped on an already weakened piece, and thereafter hurtled helplessly with it, down the length of the wall's stud space, crashing to its death?

Whichever, the incident put Bart on edge for the remainder of the night and he slept accordingly. But even though it was his second unsatisfactory night's rest in a row, and he was beginning to feel it, he was up at his usual time.

Bart was a man of habit. He awakened at precisely six-forty-five each workday. This allowed him ample time for bathing, reading *The New York Times*, which was delivered to his front door, and downing a light breakfast of coffee, black with no sugar, and two slices of toast or, as a special treat, English muffins.

Good weather or bad, he walked to work, scheduling himself to be at his desk by eight-thirty sharp. The walk gave him the exercise he needed to stay trim, kept him out of the subway which he loathed, and guaranteed him the daily moment's privacy which he cherished. The half hour before the others arrived for work, he used to get a jump on the day, as well as to make a few inroads into the mountain of financial publications that accumulated on his desk each day. Whenever he was forced to deviate from this routine, for whatever reason, it was certain to throw him off stride and into a foul humor.

When Bart came downstairs Wednesday morning, he found that not one of the traps had been violated during the night. Although disappointed, he was not all that surprised. He was accustomed to the deviousness of mice, their uncanny skill at getting their pursuers to look the other way. This one was only acting true to form. But as long as a shred of doubt remained, Bart was of no mind to fall for that old ruse. He would err on the side of caution and keep at it.

And so, that evening and the next, Bart freshened the bait, tested the traps, put them back where they were, and settled in to wait. If there was a mouse, at some point, it would have no choice but to come out to feed. He must be patient, give the traps time to do their work.

Friday morning, Bart awoke to brilliant and an outlook to match. It was going to be a halcyon day. Everything pointed to it.

The heat wave had finally broken during the night. There had been no alarming dreams to torment him. Better still, there had not been the slightest indication of life in either walls or ceiling. As a result, he had just completed his first solid night's rest since the weekend. And not a moment too soon. He needed a clear head for the meeting now a matter of hours away.

Bart attacked his morning ritual hurriedly, yet with precision, going to pains to choose a suit in which he would not only feel comfortable and at ease, but also that would be flattering to him, in this case making him appear older than he was. He selected a favorite tie "for luck," gave his shoes an extra slap with the polishing cloth for good measure, checked for overall effect in the full-length mirror, approved of what was there, and headed for the kitchen to check the traps.

For the third successive night, none had been touched. Bart had the confirmation he wanted. Immediately he set off for the bank, buoyed that this must also be a good omen, that his crucial presentation would go equally well.

Bart toyed with changing his plans. He and Meg had figured that with the Fourth of July weekend making this such a shortened workweek, the long and expensive trip to Maine would not be worth it. But now, with a resoundingly triumphant presentation behind him and the mouse episode a thing of the past, he was in the mood for a change of scene.

By midafternoon, however, his euphoria had begun to give way to the nervous drain the week's tension had exacted from him. He settled on staying in the city, perhaps eating a good dinner at a restaurant near the office, but in any case, getting to bed early.

"What a great day!" he exclaimed appreciatively to himself when he reached home around nine that evening. He pulled the key from his pocket and slid it into the lock in the front door under the stoop. Not since Monday had the house felt so welcoming to him.

He checked on the traps in the kitchen, just in case. As he expected, they were undisturbed. He decided to put off dismantling them until the next day, suddenly impatient to telephone Meg and share his abundance of good news with her.

They must have talked an hour.

"Jesus, Meg, darling! We've used up half a plane fare with this call," he said with a light laugh.

"I know"—her voice had a smile in it—"and it's been worth every cent." Bart thought so, too.

That night, the mouse struck.

Saturday morning revealed not one, but all four traps sprung and stripped bare. But there was no mouse carcass anywhere.

"Oh, goddammit to hell!" Bart stared at the traps in disbelief, torn between contradictory feelings of relief and apprehension.

On the one hand, Bart was grateful. The mystery had been resolved; he had not been "seeing things." And besides that, he had persevered and won. He had forced his adversary to commit itself, not in some wall or ceiling where Bart could not get at it, but in the open, where he could. But then, on the other, nothing like this had happened to him before in all his experience, extensive as it was. Never had these many traps been violated and not one body to show for it.

Theory followed theory, but few stood up. The most durable was that there must have been more than one mouse involved. History *could* be repeating itself. Yet Bart was absolutely certain he had not seen more than one come in. And the Dutch door had not been opened since that fateful night.

In the end, he wrote it off to his own uncertainty having dulled his cutting edge. He had simply failed to exercise the degree of care and dexterity so essential to success. The mouse had been lucky.

He put the past aside and, with renewed will, got down to the business of rearming the traps.

He worked without haste, thinking through every step, triggering each with the hairline precision of the expert he was. The bait platform fairly quivered in readiness. He spread a network of honey all about, a spur-of-the-moment addition, thinking it could serve admirably as an improvised pathfinder, like the lead wire to an explosive charge. Done, he stepped back and surveyed his work from the hall door with the satisfaction of someone who had been this route many, many times before and damn well knew what he was about.

Even though it was Saturday, he spent the day at the office. However much work he got through during the week, there was always more. He and a bank colleague, who had been plowing through a similar avalanche of paper work on his own desk, teamed up for supper and a movie afterward. The evening kept Bart from dwelling on the mouse. Or was it mice? Whichever, it was a needed and welcome respite.

Bart was home by a little after half past ten and went immediately to the kitchen to check on the condition of the traps. No mouse in any of them, but they were poised for its nightly assault, should it decide to mount one.

Preparing himself for bed, he switched on the television to catch what was left of the ten o'clock news and was pleased to see that Geraldo Rivera was on. He liked him and the human-interest features which were his specialty. Untying his shoes, he sat on the end of the bed to watch.

Rivera was interviewing a distraught young woman. She had a strong Spanish accent and cradled an infant in her arms. It appeared to be one of those child-abuse situations and Bart wondered what on earth would possess parents to batter their children. He took an immediate dislike to the young woman for what she had done or allowed to be done by someone else.

The camera panned the room, pausing by cracks in the plaster, a drooping slab of ceiling, a basin stained with rust from a still-dripping faucet and a toilet without a seat. Three small children, looking to be no more than a year apart, sat huddled at one end of a dilapidated sofa, staring wanly into the camera, mouths agape, hands dutifully folded in their laps, legs stiffly outstretched. Into view came a baby's crib, gaily decorated with characters from *Mother Goose* and smeared everywhere with deep red streaks and stains.

What monsters, Bart thought. The wretched baby was lucky to be alive. The camera continued on its gruesome journey, zooming in on a hole in the mattress. The floor could be clearly seen through it.

"You say a rat got into the baby's crib?"

"*Si! Si!* A beeg, beeg, rat. *Si, senor. Mi pobre nene!*"

"Jesus!" Bart shuddered.

The camera closed in again, this time on the baby's face. Not an inch had been spared. The upper lip was split. A large, round hole that was still oozing had been gnawed into the cheek. The left eye was swollen shut. The baby looked drugged. Bart hoped it was.

"Oh-h-h-h, *pobre, pobre*...mi *pobre nina. Que dolor por todos nosotros!*" the pathetic mother grieved, gazing down at her child, rocking it back and forth, trying to comfort it. The woman's exhausted eyes, each sunken in a black hole, were drained of tears. Rivera tried to console her in Spanish.

She put the baby back in its bloodied crib. The camera coursed down the tortured little body. The spindly legs thrust through oversized diapers were also lacerated by bites and claw marks, the distended stomach was scratched and tom, the tips of the tiny fingers chewed raw.

"Good God!" Bart winced, hurting at the sight.

"At West One-hundred-and-eighty-seventh Street, this is Geraldo Rivera reporting for..."

After switching off the set and the lamp on his bedside table Bart could not get to sleep. He had never encountered one on the hoof, so to speak, but like most people, he knew rats by reputation. His only direct exposure had come about several years earlier while walking up Madison Avenue. At the corner of Sixty-second Street, he had narrowly missed stepping on one, mashed at the curbside. It had given him a severe jolt, and he had reared back instinctively, only to find afterward that he could not take his eyes off it.

Though for the most part crushed flat, it still looked lethal enough, more than a match for any unwary passerby. To Bart, it had borne a striking resemblance to a shark, particularly about the bullet-shaped head, the savage teeth ready to slash to pieces all that stood in its path, and the underslung mouth into which they could be tucked when not needed. He had wondered if by chance, somewhere along their respective lines of evolution, some genes might not have touched.

A crowd had begun to gather around him, he recalled now, to gape and to share in his curiosity and wonderment.

"JESUS! That's one mean-looking son of a bitch!" ventured one observer, saying it all.

"Never knew them to come down this far," another.

"Me neither. Think of them more up in Harlem, places like that," a third.

"Yeah. I'll tell you something, though. If I didn't know better, I'd swear that son of a bitch was about to get up from there and come after one of us."

All in all, it had been a chilling experience for Bart who, for some unknown reason, had felt something of a personal involvement with the rat. Long after, he could still picture the leering look in its glazed eye and the open, sneering mouth, as if the rat were laughing at him over something that it knew which he didn't. Only recently had he succeeded in obliterating all vestige of it.

THREE

MONDAY MORNING, the kitchen was flooded.

"Oh, for Pete's sake, *now* what?" Bart exploded in exasperation.

A thin layer of water had spread from the front of the clothes washer, covering the area between the island counter and stainless-steel double sink, and over to the dishwasher. Bart could not tell whether the tide was expanding or receding, nor could he readily ascertain the source.

"Christ! What a way to start the week!" he muttered angrily, reaching for his address book.

Vital to the smooth functioning of a town house in New York is the strength of its underlying support systems, that band of hearty specialists who can be thrown into the breach in an emergency: roofers, electricians, glaziers, masons, and plumbers. Bart had started putting his team together literally the day he and Meg had moved in and he had been honing, polishing, and refining it ever since.

Generally speaking, he was satisfied with it, with the nagging exception of a reliable plumber. All he had tried had proven a disappointment. Even though the one he eventually settled on stood head and shoulders above the rest, he detested having to call on him now. His heart sank still further when it was other than he who answered his telephone.

"Uh...oh...hello?" Bart stumbled, taken aback by a voice he did not recognize. "I was calling...Is this...?"

"Nope. Not here," the voice did not let him finish, having encountered Bart's reaction before.

"Oh?"

"That's right."

"Any idea what time he'll be back?"

"August."

"August!" Bart could not conceal his annoyance.

"That's what I said. August."

"Damn!"

"How's that?"

Bart could sense that this was doomed to be another unhappy relationship. He weighed quitting while ahead, trying another, but decided not to. The odds were it would be no improvement.

"Uh...nothing," Bart corrected himself, trying not to lose him. "Then I take it he's asked you to cover for him while he's away?"

"You take it right. What can I do you for?"

"I've got a flood in my kitchen. Water all over the..."

"That's not good," the man said lugubriously, adding an appreciative chuckle over his understatement. "Got any notion what's the reason?"

"Could be a lot of things, but..."

"I daresay it could at that. Now, let's see what we've got here." Through the telephone, Bart could hear the pages of a book being flipped. "Let's see, let's see..."

"You know, I'm just around the comer from you..."

"Thursday looks pretty good. How about ten-thirty?"

"Thursday! You're putting me on. Didn't you hear a word I've been saying? I've got a flood on my hands and you talk about Thursday…three whole days from now?"

"Sorry, but that's the best I can do for you."

"Look! You've got to do better. Please!" Bart was having to grovel and he hated the man for it. "I'm just around the corner, as I said. It would only require a minute for you …"

"Maybe…uh…" There was more rustling of pages.

Bart could sense him weakening, decided to throw in some flattery to keep the pressure on and rising. "You know, the only reason I'm being so insistent is that I need someone really good…who really knows his stuff…and I know that Bill would never tolerate anyone who wasn't absolutely tops covering for him…people he deals with wouldn't stand for anything but the best."

"Right around the corner, you say?"

Ten, fifteen, twenty minutes crept by; then half an hour since the man had said with the finality of an airline pilot at takeoff, "I'll be right over." Bart was beginning to worry that something had gone wrong. Frequent checks of the water level in the kitchen had failed to reveal either an improving or a worsening situation. Tim had eased some of the urgency, but even in the best of times, Bart was not one to take being kept waiting with grace. No sooner had he stopped expecting it, than the doorbell rang.

"Good morning, sir!" said the middle-aged man who looked down at him from the top of the stoop, showing not the least sign of remorse at having left Bart hanging close to an hour.

"Glad you're here," Bart exuded nonetheless, forgetting in his relief the irritation that had built to boiling. "This way…down here."

"Oh?" There was disappointment in the man's face. "I sort of got the impression from the way you were talking on the phone that this was your own place," he complained.

"It is." Bart laughed, understanding. "But you see, we have two entrances. This is the one we use most of the time. Besides, the kitchen is on this floor and so it's easier to get to it through here."

"Oh." The man went along, but obviously without much conviction, reluctantly descending the steps, not taking his puzzled eyes off Bart. "Pleased to meet you," he announced, thrusting his right hand into Bart's and sweeping authoritatively past him, into the house. "Mighty nice place," looking to the right and left as he advanced.

"Thanks. We like it," Bart accepted the compliment, but in a tone to discourage further familiarity.

"When's the last time someone ran these machines?"

"I did. Last night."

"Which?"

"Clothes washer."

"Fits."

"Why?"

"Water. Soapy." The plumber had dipped the tips of his fingers into the water on the floor and was running his thumb across them, back and forth. "Hazy look to it, too, grayish-like. See what I mean?" he invited Bart to squat alongside for closer inspection.

"Yes. Yes, I do. I hadn't noticed that before, to tell the truth," Bart said admiringly. He liked the man's refreshing, get-right-to-the-point approach.

"Well, I'll lay you my bottom dollar on it...one of them, anyway," he inserted with a smile, "problem's got something to do with that machine."

"That's a relief...I suppose," Bart said, rising, the backs of his legs starting to cramp. "Will it be hard to fix, do you think?" he asked with trepidation, still expecting the usual mumbo-jumbo he was accustomed to getting from plumbers.

"Shouldn't be. But can't know for sure. Trouble is, any damn fool can tell you where the problem is, but that's about as good as nothing at all until you know what's causing it. And that, my friend, is how you separate a sheep from a goat, like they say," laughing lightly.

"I guess it is at that," Bart joined in, both impressed and pleasantly surprised by the ingenuousness of the man. "Can I give you a hand with the thing?"

"Could use one," the plumber accepted. "They can be a little ornery about it sometimes."

Each grabbing a side, they heaved and coaxed the machine down its narrow niche, away from the back wall, inching it into open space. Progress was slow. Bart worried about losing his grip and getting his fingers smashed between the washer and the dryer next to it.

"Been having a little mouse trouble, I see," the plumber said offhandedly, as though to make polite conversation while they worked.

"Uh..." Bart wondered how he knew. "Oh! Oh, yes," he acknowledged, remembering about the traps he had left on the island counter, cleaned, ready for baiting and redeployment.

"They can be a terrible nuisance, that's for damn sure."

"I know. This one's been a real pain in the ass. I've been after it for a week already and the other night it sprang all four traps and stole the bait right off them."

"Sounds to me like maybe you got more than one. This'll do fine," the plumber said, releasing his side of the machine and moving to the back of it. "Yup! Just like I thought."

"What?"

"Here's what," the plumber said, pointing at a small, jagged stub of black neoprene hose poking through the rear panel. "This here's the drain hose...or what's left of it, anyhow."

"Oh?"

"That's a fact. What makes you so sure it's only one?" the plumber asked, continuing his examination of the machine.

"One what?" Bart responded distractedly, his attention held by the mutilated hose stub.

"Mouse, of course!" the plumber answered somewhat impatiently.

"Oh...uh...well, I only saw one come in from the garden. *That* much I'm sure of, anyway."

"Hard to figure," the plumber said.

"I know," Bart agreed, thinking they were talking about the same thing, saw they weren't. The plumber had removed the stub of hose from the machine and was examining it closely, rolling it slowly between his fingers. "What do you think?"

"Like I say, hard to figure."

"I mean, the machine's not that old, you know," Bart volunteered defensively.

"I can tell," the plumber agreed. "Been taken good care of, too. You can see that."

"So, what's the verdict, doctor?"

"Sometimes the casing starts out weak and the heat gets to be too much for it and then BANG! you got yourself a busted drain hose."

"Jesus! You'd think they'd put better-quality stuff in these things. Not exactly cheap this baby, as I recall," Bart observed, feeling he had once again been victimized by forced obsolescence.

"You'd think," the plumber agreed. "Still and all, look at it this way. If the manufacturer was to use better material, then it'd last longer and there'd be nothing left out there for guys like me...no way to make a buck. So, it's not all bad, right?" he observed in mock seriousness.

"Oh, I get it," Bart played along. "One guy's loss is the other's gain. Is that what you're saying?"

"Something like that."

"Well, thanks a lot!" Bart said, chuckling. "Look!" he had turned suddenly serious. "Mind if I ask you a question?"

"Why not?"

"It's something that's been eating at me. Don't think I've lost my marbles. Okay?"

"I usually can spot them that has before this... and so far, there's been no sign," the plumber said with a twinkle in his eye.

"'That's good to know. But seriously... uh... do you know much about rats?"

"*Rats?*"

"Yes. Rats."

"Little as possible... and believe you me, I try to keep it that way. Why? What's on your mind?"

"Well, I was wondering... uh..." Bart hesitated, as though anticipating the answer and wanting to hold it in abeyance for as long as possible. Then he blurted, "In your opinion, could a rat have caused this?"

"You mean chewed a hole in the hose and..."

"Exactly."

"Could. No doubt about that. Even looks kind of chewed. But just as likely a bunch of mice, too. Not just one. But a mess of them could with no trouble. What makes you come up with something like that all of a sudden?"

"Not all that all of a sudden, but anyway, the traps I was telling you about, and then the other night, I was watching this television program... Geral--"

"I should've guessed," the plumber broke in heatedly. "That's the trouble with this country today. Too goddam much television. We let it do all our thinking for us. Terrible. Just terrible."

"This was a news program" Bart continued defensively, "but anyway, that doesn't answer the question."

"Well, like I say, I don't know all that much about the buggers, but it seems to me it wouldn't take any kind of genius to figure out if he's got one in his house or not."

"I guess that's what I'm asking. How *do* you know?"

"Place gets torn to pieces, for one thing. And then, they just about eat you out of house and home while they're at it. Anything like that been happening around here?"

"No. Not really. Not that I've seen."

"Well then!" he said triumphantly. "Sounds to me like you've answered your own question." The plumber had taken out a long piece of fiber-reinforced hose from his toolbox, slid one end onto the appropriate nozzle on the back of the machine and was securing it with a metal clamp. "Better than the original," he said proudly.

"That's good," Bart thanked him.

The plumber fed the hose's other end through a hole in the floor, at the base of the back wall, evidently cut there to accommodate its predecessor.

"There!" he said, leaning into the machine, shoving it by himself into its customary location. "You're all set."

"What a relief! I was starting to fear the worst."

"No sweat! Should be good as new. Better, even."

"Not that... I mean, it's great about the machine and all that... but also what you say about not being a rat."

"Oh, that. Yes, well, from the sound of it, the only mistake you've been making, seems to me, is being so all-fired sure there's only one."

"You're probably right."

"I hope so for your sake. Anyway, if it was me, I'd hold on to thinking that way until I had some good reason not to."

"I hear you."

"And then, I'd get myself as many goddam traps as I thought I needed... six, eight, ten even...so I could put them all over the goddam house... wherever I'd been hearing them or figured they'd go...that kind of thing."

He plugged in the machine, turned it on and ran it through its cycles, rotating its on/off knob rapidly in order to accelerate the process.

"From what you say—"

"What?" Bart interrupted, unable to hear over the noise.

"I was saying"—louder—"from what you've been telling me, that's what I'd do. Machine's working fine. Notice?"

"Yes. Yes, I do. Thanks a lot."

"And you'll see. You'll wrap it up in no time. Use plenty of bait...make them have to spend some time to get all of it off. You'll nail 'em sure."

Bart thought about recounting his own experiences with mice, but decided there was no point.

The plumber stopped the washer, using its top to do some calculations on the back of an invoice pad. He flipped it over, filled in the numbers, ripped off the sheet and handed it to Bart.

"Are you sure that's enough?" taken aback.

"One thing about me. I never charge less than the job's worth, but never more, either."

"Fair enough," Bart agreed with a smile. "Who shall I make it out to?" He removed a blank check from his wallet.

"To 'Cash,' if it's all the same to you."

"No problem at all," Bart agreed pleasantly, starting to fill out the check as requested.

"Saves me from having to share it with Uncle Sam later on, if you see what I'm saying," the plumber explained with a conspiratorial leer.

"Yes, I do. Not hard to understand, either...not these days, anyway."

"You better believe it. The way taxes have gotten, there's almost no point in working anymore. Anyhow, you can call me anytime you got some extra business to throw around, okay?" he requested, folding Bart's check into one compartment of his wallet and pulling forth his business card from another. "I'm nice and close by in the neighborhood, too."

"So I see. You can count on it," Bart said with feeling, for he knew that the final piece of his support system had fallen into place at last.

Bart was glad that he had made himself ask the question about the possibility of a rat. The plumber had struck him as a man who would know about such things and, sure enough, he had. To have him issue his verdict so unreservedly had lifted an enormous burden from Bart's shoulders.

Ever since Geraldo Rivera's disturbing feature report, so close on the heels of what had been done to the four traps, Bart's fertile imagination had given him no peace, working on him like a gathering storm. By Sunday, twenty-four hours later, his jitters over what he might be up against had become so virulent that he was compelled even to shut his bedroom door.

Walking home from the office Monday evening, he adhered to the plumber's advice and picked up an additional eight traps. Combined with those he had, this would give him an even dozen to work with. They should suffice.

He loaded them extra generously, some with cheese, others with peanut butter, still others with chunks of bread soaked in honey. After augmenting the number to five in the kitchen, where he still thought he had his best shot, he was left with enough traps to place one in each room of the house, including two in his own bedroom.

Come one, come all. He was ready.

FOUR

The night raised more questions than it answered.

The mice made not a sound throughout. No running about, no scratching, nothing. Bart was certain of this, for his sleep had never extended beyond surface depth. The slightest disturbance, had there been any, would surely have snapped him out of it instantly.

And yet they had been busy, very busy. Altogether, eight traps on four floors had been hit, sprung and stripped bare, but not one had exacted the extreme penalty.

More puzzling still, the four traps that had been rejected were each one of them baited with peanut butter. These included two of those in the kitchen and one in his bedroom. In the past, it had been the peanut butter which had worked every time after all else had failed.

Bart spent the day at the office waiting impatiently for it to end, so that the night could start. He was burning with curiosity to see what it would bring and pondered what refinements he should apply to baiting and deploying the traps to better his chances.

But before he could actually get down to it, he had to

make good on a dinner engagement of long standing. It was something Meg had arranged for him prior to her departure for the summer. "Tell him to come along, anyway," their hostess-to-be had insisted in response to Meg telling her she would be away. "We can always use an extra man." Bart had no taste for the part in the best of circumstances, and even less in the present one, but he had promised Meg he would go.

He left the earliest he could without appearing rude, reaching home shortly past ten forty-five. Bone weary, he fumbled for his key, wishing he could go straight to bed and didn't have the traps yet to do. A police car rumbled slowly past, spilling its headlights into where he was standing under the stoop, momentarily alleviating the aloneness suddenly engulfing him. As he pushed open the door, a nerve-shattering series of clackety-clacks broke the forbidding stillness flowing out of the house. Bart sprang back.

"Who's there?" he croaked, hardly able to find voice. "I said, who's there, goddammit?" It came out stronger, but was more to gain the companionship of a friendly sound than in anticipation of a response. He considered running after the police car, but resisted for fear of its being nothing and he appearing a fool.

Far off, he heard the heavy, muted tha-lump...tha-lump of someone methodically descending a flight of stairs. He assumed they were the footsteps of a neighbor. Thank the Lord they were home. As the headlights had before, the sounds made him feel less alone, that in case of real emergency there was someone not too far he could call on. Then he remembered. The houses were empty, both families, like his, gone for their summer holidays until after Labor Day. "Oh, my God!"

Bart forced himself through the doorway, his heart

pounding. The house was suffocating, deathly still. What could it have been? If a burglar, where would he be hiding? Bart pushed on, his mouth dry, his eyes wide, his breath shallow and labored.

He reached for the wall switch, feeling a little easier when the hall light came on. Purposely he left the front door open, assuring his escape route, if it came to that. Reaching the doorway to the kitchen, he glided his right hand around it, felt for the switch, flicked it on.

"Anybody there?"

Silence.

He stepped into the kitchen and proceeded ever so slowly past the stainless-steel double sink to the door which gave access to the playroom in the basement. It was closed. In all likelihood, the prowler would be lurking on the other side, down the darkened stairwell.

After a moment's hesitation, Bart grabbed the doorknob and turned it cautiously but firmly until it could go no further. Readying himself to slam into the intruder the instant he bolted out, thereby smashing him against the wall, Bart threw open the door.

"Come out of there, goddam you!"

Silence. Bart waited, straining to hear breathing, anything. Nothing.

He felt around the corner with his right hand, his fingers stretching, feeling, crawling toward the wall switch. Something brushed against it, softly, no more than a tickle. He yanked it back, his head now pounding. He feared the top of it might blow off. Recovering, leaning slightly on the doorway, he tried anew, pressing his hand more firmly against the wall this time, creeping, reaching. Finally, he had it. The light came on, he craned his neck cautiously around the doorframe.

Three-quarters down the stairs lay the same mop Bart

had used in vain to flush the mouse from under the clothes washer and which he had subsequently left on the landing to air and dry. It had lost its footing and toppled headlong the length of the staircase, its stiff handle slapping each bare wooden step as it proceeded.

In both relief and anger, he hurled the dustcloth, which had been hanging by the wall switch and had given him such an additional turn, down the stairwell after it.

"Good Christ, what a terrible day!" he grumbled aloud emphatically, taking it out on the door by slamming it shut.

Although he felt even less like it now than when he had first arrived, he knew he must attend to the traps. It required in excess of a half hour to retrieve, clean and load them all, this time skipping the peanut butter. He distributed them pretty much as before except for a heavier concentration on the two bottom floors and none in his bedroom. No sense in killing the mice at his bedside if it wasn't necessary.

Bart hadn't spoken with Meg since Friday, four long days ago. He felt her absence keenly and decided to call her, despite the hour. She answered midway through the first ring.

"That was quick. I hope I didn't wake you."

"It wouldn't have made the slightest difference if you had. I was hoping it might be you. How are you, my love?"

Hearing her voice acted like a tonic on him, infusing him with new life.

"I just had the living daylights scared out of me, as a matter of fact," he said and proceeded to tell her what had just occurred.

"Thank God that's all it was." Meg sighed. "To be honest, I sometimes worry about you being all alone in that house, that something like a real burglar...well, better not to dwell on that gloomy possibility, wouldn't you say?"

"Agreed. But I thought you'd be interested. Anyway, all is well." Neither spoke for a moment, then Bart continued. "Speaking of gloomy, it turns out we *do* have mice after all, and from the looks of things, we must have a whole raft of them."

"Oh, Bart, no!"

"Afraid so, dammit! Right after you and I talked last Friday? That's when they made their move. During the night. All four traps got hit."

"What rotten luck!"

"I know. It crossed my mind that it could be a rat."

"What on earth made you think that?"

Bart recounted all that had been happening, how the mice had struck a second time, springing eight of the twelve traps, the coincidence of the burst drain hose, and the lingering effects of seeing that wretched child on television.

"Bart, don't you think you should call the exterminator, just to play it safe, to be absolutely sure?" Meg suggested worriedly.

"I suppose I could, but I don't know any."

"What about the Yellow Pages?"

"I guess what I'm saying is I feel perfectly capable of handling the problem myself."

"Yes, I must say, it isn't that you haven't had enough experience, God knows. Maybe you're right. Still..."

"Besides, what the hell can an exterminator do that's different from what I would do? Seems to me, our objective is the same, only the method is different, maybe."

"Well, suit yourself, darling. It's you with the problem. But if it was me..."

"Look at it this way, sweetheart. I enjoy the challenge.

Why give it to someone else and let them have all the fun?" he asked, not entirely facetiously.

"Oh, Bart, you're too much," Meg laughed affectionately before saying good-bye.

Four hours later, after Bart had gone to bed, a resounding crash echoed through the house. Downstairs something heavy had free-fallen or been knocked to the floor. Bart's eyes popped open, his mind made up about the cause. Instantaneously, he decided what to do.

Quickly, he swung his legs over the side of the bed and tiptoed toward the hall outside his bedroom, pausing only long enough to grab a heavy work boot from his closet. If he got the chance to club some of them dead, he didn't want to miss it.

Reaching the banister, he craned his neck over it. He could vaguely make out the ground floor through the open staircase. The house was black as a tomb and utterly still.

He thought of switching on the overhead lights, but decided not to. His eyes were surprisingly well adjusted to the dark and he was able to see far more clearly than he would have thought possible. As important, he figured his chances of success would be immeasurably bettered if he could sneak up on the mice from behind, catch them unaware, before they could dart back into an inaccessible hiding place.

Grasping the railing for both support and direction, he started down, his boot in his right hand. Suddenly a stair landing squeaked underfoot. Instinctively, he drew back, stopped dead. "Don't *do* that!" he hissed down at it; through clenched teeth, not daring to advance until confident the noise had not carried. He stepped over the offending stair to the one below it. Finally, he arrived at the vestibule on the second floor, tiptoed across it, again craned his neck over the banister, listened. All was quiet, but then signs of movement in the kitchen, muffled, spasmodic, a kind of rustling. Bart's heart accelerated, the pounding in his head worsened. Squeezing both banister and boot until his knuckles whitened, he resumed the descent.

Another stair landing creaked under him. He stopped in his tracks.

"You hear that?" It was a man's voice, in a stage whisper. A beam of light ignited, shot out of the kitchen, into the hallway.

The terror that swept through Bart was unimaginable. His stomach turned upside down. He thought he might vomit and swallowed hard to avoid it.

"Yeah"—another stage whisper—"think so." The flashlight sprayed the hall below.

Bart was paralyzed with fear, incapable of moving. Finding a strength he didn't know was within him, he snapped out of it and literally flew up the stairs, back to his bedroom, straight to the telephone on Meg's desk. Maybe if he could alert the police, there might yet be time to reach him, before it was too late.

Heavy footsteps started to clump up the carpeted staircase.

Clutching the receiver in his left hand, he fumbled for the dial with his other, fumbled to find the "0," spun it, deliberately slowing its return to keep the noise down.

"Give me the police!" he rasped in a whisper as loud as he dared, even before he had the receiver to his mouth. "Hurry! For God's sake, hurry! PLEASE!"

But the line was dead. Oh, dear God, it couldn't be. Not now. With despair verging on hysteria, he jammed the plunger into the cradle again and again, harder and harder.

But nothing doing. My God! He realized they had cut the line.

Bart bathed in an icy sweat, wanted desperately to run, to find a place to hide. But where? He thought of the closet, but rejected the idea. It was likely to be the first place they would want to empty. The memory of a friend at the bank, telling him of waking up one night to find burglars in his bedroom, flashed into his head. His advice: stay put, play dead, let them help themselves. He hadn't, and came close to being done in as a result, the police rescuing him only at the eleventh hour.

Bart dove for his bed, pulled the sheet high over his head, and waited.

The footsteps neared.

Bart could not recall ever having been so utterly consumed by terror. He burrowed deeper into the mattress. He had paid a king's ransom to have his house wired against just this sort of contingency. Where were those useless sons of bitches now, the one time he had needed their protection? He thought his head or his heart, or both, might explode.

From under the sheet, he could discern the glow of the flashlight sweeping the room. The man holding it was so close, Bart could hear his rapid breathing, evidence of the exertion it had taken him to climb to the third floor. Or was Bart mistaking the other's for his own?

"Hey!" the man called to his partner. "Here's the dude." The light showing through the sheet had brightened considerably. Bart knew the flashlight was aimed straight at him.

"Where?" asked the second, running down the hall from where he was, in Bart junior's bedroom.

"Here!" said the first. "Under the sheet there."

"Good! Okay, let's--"

Bart did not let the second man finish, damned if he was simply going to lie there and wait to be hit on the head. He threw the sheet to one side, sat up, struggling to speak. "Wait! Wait!" he managed to blurt out. "Take anything you want! Help yourselves! Really! Anything!"

"Take it easy there, buddy," said the one pointing the flashlight into Bart's face.

"No, no, I mean it. Listen to me...anything. Take it! I won't say a word. Promise."

"Hey! You gotta get hold of yourself. You the owner?"

"Yes. Yes, I am...so you see, you *can* have it...whatever you like," Bart answered.

"You don't understand, mister," said the one holding the flashlight, for the first time removing it from Bart's eyes. "We've been sent to investigate a break in your line. Security Alarm Systems. See?" He shone the flashlight onto his partner's uniform, illuminating the bright yellow shoulder patch with the dark blue crossed pistols and bold SAS woven into it, and onto the shiny gold badge pinned above the breast pocket of his shirt.

"I thought for sure you..." Bart started softly, beginning to recover.

"Yeah. We didn't exactly know who you were either... when we thought we heard somebody moving around upstairs awhile back."

"That's right," confirmed the other, buttoning the leather strap that secured his pistol into its holster. "Better being safe than sorry, in our line of work," he said with a smile, patting the butt of the gun. "Sure didn't mean to be shaking you up so bad."

"That's okay," Bart said quietly, still in shock.

"Anyway, like I was saying. There's been a break in your line. Showed up at Central. Mind if we keep looking? Had to be something."

"No, no. By all means. I'll be right with you," Bart said, getting out of bed. His knees felt rubbery.

The two men climbed to the fourth floor, looked into closets, checked windows and the central skylight over the stairwell. By their return past his bedroom door, Bart was dressed and ready to fall in step.

"Nothing so far," announced the one leading the way.

"Yeah. Kinda hard to explain...unless there's a problem in the phone," agreed the other.

"Oh?" Bart asked, ears perking.

"Yeah. Our system ties into the phone company's, you know. And sometimes when things go wrong with their equipment, it screws up ours."

"Well, the phone *is* dead, as a matter of fact," Bart said. "At least it was when I tried calling the cops about you guys...I mean, when I thought you were prowlers," he explained, a note of apology in his voice.

"That a fact? Could be it."

They had arrived at the kitchen.

"Jesus! No wonder the phone don't work. Line's been cut clean in two," the man kneeling in the corner said to his partner and Bart, both now hovering over his shoulder.

"Goddam mice!" Bart reacted angrily, thinking aloud.

"Mister! This is no mouse that's done this to you. No way. More'n likely a rat."

"Oh, my God!" Bart gasped.

"Look how much of the line's missing...every bit of three feet, be my guess. It'd take an army of mice to put all that away. And see all these here?"

"Yes," Bart said.

The man had picked up a pellet from the many strewn about on the floor under the control box. It was dark brown, almost black, and was shaped more or less like a grain of rice, although of a different texture and slightly larger.

"Them's rat droppings," the man announced solemnly. "And from the feel of 'em, they haven't been here long." He squashed the one he held between his thumb and forefinger flat. "See?" he thrust it toward Bart. "Feel for yourself!"

"I'll take your word for it, thanks," Bart rejected the offer, grimacing.

"So, there's your answer. We'll make out our report and..."

"I guess I'm not all that surprised really," Bart said resignedly.

"That so?"

"Yes. The guy's been hitting my traps, stealing the bait. Then, I'm sure he was involved in a busted drain hose I had. And now this."

"And that's not all," the man's partner said from across the room. Bart had not noticed him move, but he was standing by the double sink, holding the toaster.

Its electrical cord had been viciously mutilated, a savage wound gouged in its flank, exposing its innards along a broad expanse. It was holding in one piece by no more than a few copper strands and what was left of its thin neoprene skin.

"And Christ only knows what else he's gotten into around the house," the same man observed ruefully. "Not much stands in their way."

Bart was too numbed by events to react more than to say, "I feel like such a fool. How could I have been so stupid...kidding myself like that, wasting time?"

"Take it easy on yourself," the first man said. "How could you know? Now you do, though, you can do something about it, right? But I'll tell you something, you can't get anywhere using dinky little peashooters like this." He was holding one of the traps. "What you need is honest-to-God ones for rats."

"So stupid," Bart chided himself again, shaking his head.

"You go out today and buy yourself some rat traps and you'll be okay," the first man said, trying to comfort him.

"Do you think I should get an exterminator in?"

"Tell the truth, I don't see what one of them can do that you can't do just as good. I mean, he isn't gonna be able to catch the rat any faster'n you, you think?"

"I don't know. I guess that's why I'm asking."

"Up to you, of course, but if it was me, I'd rely on myself first, but maybe that's just me. Anyway, I guess we about done all there is to do here. We'll be making our report soon as we get to a phone...and they'll make the arrangements to see you get back in business."

"Thanks," Bart said. "But wouldn't you guys like a cup of coffee before you go? It'll be daylight soon. No sense in my trying to go back to bed at this point." Bart didn't want to be left alone.

"Sure!" they said in unison. "Appreciate it. Couple more minutes won't make that much difference."

Bart lit the flame under the kettle, dug out the jar of instant-coffee mix, and placed cups at the ready on the island counter.

"Here! Sit yourselves down!" he invited them, pulling out two chairs at the kitchen table. "Either of you fellas had much experience with rats?"

"Naw...only as we come across them in our work...in cellars and places like that. But not in our homes, like you got, if that's what you mean?"

"Yes, it is."

"But my wife's old lady, she sure as hell did," put in the one who had discovered the mutilated toaster cord.

"You never told me about that," accused his partner, a combination of surprise and hurt.

"Because the question never came up before," the storyteller defended himself. "Anyway, seems no matter what she tried, she couldn't get rid of it......nothing. Rat paid no attention to it, or seemed to like the stuff. Can you believe that? So, then she tried catching him off base, by disguising it, wrapped in big juicy chunks of raw meat, that kind of thing."

"This a true story?" his partner chuckled, sensing that his leg was about to be pulled.

"God's very own...but that didn't work either, excepting to the dog that got into it...the dumb son of a bitch. So, then she got herself a whole lot of rat traps...just like you're gonna be doing, right?"

"I'm planning to do that today, you better believe it," Bart reassured him earnestly.

"Good! So, she sets up these traps all over the goddam house...because naturally, she doesn't know where the son of a bitch is exactly...but that didn't improve the situation either. The old rat, he just went around springing them and snatching the bait and having himself a high old time...and meanwhile chewing up everything in sight, raising hell all over the place, getting into the food. Man! It was something awful. And, of course by now the old lady was getting kinda uptight about it all, you know?"

"I can imagine," Bart said.

"And I suppose I wasn't all that much help, telling her she better get her ass in gear, before he takes off after her... leastways, that's what my missus told me...but, anyhow, the old lady went out and got herself a cat...found it out back, into the garbage one day...mean as all get out. Tear your arm off, soon as look at you."

"You *sure* this is a true story?"

"You're interrupting," the storyteller cautioned his partner.

"Go on, please," Bart urged, getting up to fill the cups from the boiling kettle, and bringing them to the table.

"Well, so she turns this cat loose and you know what happens?" The two listeners looked at each other, neither volunteering. "Kills him...that's what."

"Who?" Bart asked.

"The rat," the storyteller answered.

"Goddammit!" his partner exploded in exasperation. "The cat kill the rat or the rat kill the cat?"

"No need to be shouting," the storyteller tweaked him, delighted with the rise he had gotten. "The rat killed the cat."

"You're kidding! I've never heard of such a thing," Bart marveled, so engrossed in the tale he was forgetting what was in his own house.

'Well, didn't kill him exactly, but might as well...beat him up so bad. The old lady, she had to take him to the vet, to get him sewed up, but the vet, he took one look and put a needle in him instead. And that was that, far as the cat was concerned. But that still left the problem of the rat." He put three heaping teaspoons of sugar into his cup, filled it to the brim with half-and-half, and stirred pensively.

"Speaking of which..." Bart coaxed him into resuming.

"So happens," he acquiesced, "the old lady has this boyfriend at the time. My missus and me didn't cotton to him much, but he stuck around so long, we figured he must be putting it to her the way she liked it..."

"Jesus Christ!" his partner exclaimed. "This goddam story got an end?"

"Like I was saying, she told this boyfriend of hers about the rat and what he done, and this guy...I guess he fancied himself as some kind of macho type...anyway, he tells her to leave the rat to him and for her to get the hell out of the house until he says she can come back. Then he pulls out this twelve-gauge shotgun he'd use for hunting and goes in there and has himself a time. Shot up the place pretty bad, but they never did find trace of that rat after he got done. Musta blown the son of a bitch to kingdom come. And in a matter of only a couple hours with him, too. He was really in solid with the old lady after that, so it was kind of a mixed blessing, far as me and my missus went. Walls still got pock marks in them and every now and then a piece of buckshot turns up." He was shaking his head at the recollection.

"George!" his partner said, getting up abruptly from the table, "You're full of shit!" Everybody laughed. "C'mon, George. We gotta go. Thanks for the coffee."

"I'm the one who thanks you fellas," Bart said sincerely, leading them out the downstairs door, onto the street. The sun was rising. The day promised to be a real winner.

"Say! Before I forget it," said George's partner, "you know that big bag of hamster food you got leaning up against the icebox? You can't go leaving stuff like that around...not with a rat loose."

"Oh, yes. That belongs to my daughter. She's into hamsters in a big way."

"That's okay, but you're just asking for trouble keeping it around for a hungry rat to get into. He can stay alive a long while with all of that."

"Okay, fine. Thanks. I'll do something about it right away."

"That's good...like in here..." The man smiled, tapping the metal garbage can next to him with the side of his shoe. "No half measures, hear?"

And they were gone.

Even though it flew in the face of Bart's puritanical New England upbringing to throw out a perfectly good, unopened, twenty-five-pound bag of animal food, he could certainly appreciate the soundness of the advice. He returned to the kitchen immediately to follow through on it, before he could change his mind.

The bag stood crisp and erect, catty-comer between the icebox and the wall. Bart reached over, tightening his stomach muscles the way he would instinctively when anticipating something heavy, seized the bag firmly and lifted.

It was empty. The few pellets remaining inside rolled out, through a gaping hole in the bag's backside, and pinged onto the floor.

The rat had beaten him to it.

FIVE

BART KNEW NOTHING ABOUT RATS, other than by reputation. He knew nothing about their living habits, peculiarities, how best to track and kill them, the dangers. This was no way to go into battle. That much he did know.

And so, as a start, on Wednesday he cancelled his luncheon plans at the bank and went directly to the main branch of the New York Public Library instead. He was both surprised and disappointed by how little there was available on rats, and that what there was of it seemed to be written with the country rat in mind and the farmer whose crops it was destroying. There was close to nothing for the city dweller having to combat an urban variety in his home.

Nonetheless, Bart spent the better part of that afternoon there, examining anything and everything which he thought could be even remotely applicable to his situation. As he turned in the last pamphlet at the desk, he was satisfied that he had exhausted this source.

Bart checked in at the office long enough to reassure himself that his long, unexplained absence had not led to any raised eyebrows and to check if there was anything which required immediate attention. There were none on either count. He straightened his desk, locked his file cabinet and strode out of the office.

"Gone for the day," he informed his secretary briskly.

"What shall I tell anyone who calls?" she asked, pointedly looking at her wrist watch. It was not yet four.

"Just that...and that I'll get back to them in the morning," Bart said impersonally.

"Very well, Mr. Hughes." In all the years she had worked for him, she had never known him to leave work early without telling her where he was going.

There was nothing mysterious about Bart's early departure. He had rat traps to buy, and he didn't want to risk finding stores which he thought might carry them closed by the time he got there. And he was right, but for a slightly different reason.

Rat traps, he discovered, were not a staple item in his neighborhood. As a result, he had to detour from his normal route home, and it was well past six when he finally turned wearily onto his block. He had found seven traps altogether and bought them all.

But more demoralizing than the search itself had been the running commentary from merchants that accompanied each purchase. The cumulative effect had been to erode most of the confidence Bart had labored all day to build, leaving him depressed and apprehensive. Perhaps, too, the fact that he had been on his feet since before dawn was also a contributing factor.

In any case, with each step that took him to his house, his pace slowed and his heartbeat quickened. He looked up and down the street in both directions, hoping to find someone to talk with, some excuse to defer the inevitable, but there was no one. Even the corpulent doorman of the pretentious apartment building midway down the block was away from his regular post under the awning.

Bart paused, looked at his house, so empty, cold, and forbidding. Its blackened windows gave him the illusion of staring at a gargantuan human skull. He took a deep breath, let out a long, audible sigh, drove the image away and crossed the street.

It was almost more than he could bring himself to do, to shove the key into the lock of the door under the stoop. The sound of the bolt being thrown echoed off the bare stone walls around him and into the hollow blackness where he was headed. He rotated the key another quarter turn. The latch gave, but he held the door fast, in case the rat was on the other side, waiting to pounce on him the second it had room to get through.

"Oh, Christ!" He sighed again, let the door go. Little by little, it swung free. The impression of another presence issuing from the house was so intense, he gasped in reaction to it, instinctively springing to craning his neck around the doorframe to see down one side, out of the way, and waited expectantly, the pitch-black hallway.

"Hello! I'm home!" he called into the house.

Overpowering silence returned his greeting.

Warily, he made himself enter, listening and looking all about, as taut and alert as any animal in the forest sensing imminent peril. He kept his back tightly pressed to the wall and slowly sidled into and down the empty corridor. Only a little more to go before reaching the first light switch.

All of a sudden, from off in the distance, tha-lump!... tha-lump!...tha-lump! He froze.

It was unmistakable, the identical sound as the night before. He knew now what had caused the drying mop to topple down the playroom stairs.

He held his breath, waited in the black stillness, thinking that it might recur. It didn't. His mind raced to decide what to do next. Where was that goddam wall switch? He groped for it, dove for where he thought it should be. There! Had it. Thank God! The light came on, brilliantly, flickered and was gone.

"Oh, goddammit!" Bart cried out, as though in physical pain. "Why now, goddam you?" he cursed the burned-out bulb.

The rat was in the stairwell. There could be no doubt. It consisted of at least twenty steps. Yet Bart had heard only three tha-lumps. This could be his chance.

He ran for the clothes closet, clawed his way through it until he found what he wanted, an umbrella with a heavy wooden handle. It would do well as a club. He raced toward the stairwell, pausing only long enough to throw on the kitchen lights. He was panting like a steam engine.

"Oh, Jesus!" The stairwell door was closed.

It was a bad piece of luck, but he never broke stride, wrenching it open without hesitation, weapon raised and at the ready. He flicked on the light at the top of the stairs and cautiously started his descent.

Step by careful step he went, expecting at any moment to discover the rat cowering in the comer of one of them. He reached bottom.

Exhilaration had supplanted his earlier trepidation. He couldn't wait to do battle. Bart could almost hear the rat breathing from somewhere in the room.

He reached around the corner, tripped the switch for the overhead lights. Suddenly, the room was bathed in a bluish, fluorescent hue. He stepped off the bottom ledge.

Methodically, he undertook the search. Holding the umbrella by its handle now, he used the tip to probe into the stacks of toys abandoned everywhere, to sweep under the furniture, and to investigate every suspicious corner. He was confident the rat would make a break for it, and when it did, that would be its end, impaled on the tip of his umbrella.

But the rat guarded its secret jealously, making not a sound, waiting for the storm to pass.

"Okay, you son of a bitch, this round's yours," Bart granted it after almost ten minutes of fruitless search. He felt the disappointment keenly. "But mark my word, wherever the hell you are, the next one's mine."

Back in the kitchen, Bart shook the contents of the brown paper bag onto the island counter and picked up the last trap to fall out. This was his first opportunity to study one at close range. It was an awesome thing, built along the lines of a mouse trap, to be sure, but so much bigger, so much more threatening.

He tested the spring for tension. The further back he pulled it, the greater it resisted him. He decided to try for the distance, to cock it. It produced in him the same gnawing malaise as when handling a loaded pistol, the same fear that the slightest misstep could cause it to go off accidentally. Delicately, he fastened the retaining hook over the leading edge of the spring. Sitting there on the island counter, the trap looked as if a passing breeze would suffice to detonate it. Its shiny, copper bait platform was trembling nervously. And so, he noticed, were his hands.

Bart gave himself a few minutes, then seized the trap by the base, relying only on his thumb and forefinger to do so. The others he curled against the inside of his hand. Gently, so gently, he lowered his lethal cargo to the floor, heaving a giant sigh of relief once he had it safely there and his hand clear.

Holding an old leather leash by its loop handle, he let the metal clasp fall slowly toward the trap. Bart was standing to one side, using the island counter as both support and shield. Lower and lower, he let the clasp drop, feeling for the bait platform with no more weight than that of a feather.

Suddenly, when he thought he still had a way to go, the trap exploded with a resonant CRACK!, as crisp as a rifle shot. It leapt three feet off the floor, closing on the metal clasp as would a fish catching an insect on the wing. Instinctively, Bart jumped back even though in no danger.

"Watch and weep, you rotten bastard," he called down the playroom stairs. "One of these babies has your name on it." His spirits were lifting.

Bart required another half dozen or so practice runs at cocking, gaining welcome self-assurance with each. Then he felt ready to load in earnest.

Since the rat had rejected the mouse traps baited with peanut butter, he decided to limit himself to cheddar cheese alone. He also thought that to use all seven traps bordered on overkill. Besides, he liked holding something in reserve whenever feasible. Five should be adequate.

He placed one in the kitchen in front of the clothes washer, one each in the library and living room and two in the playroom. Surveying his work, there was cause to be optimistic. The enemy had been identified at last and Bart had the proper artillery mounted against it. The end should be in sight.

It had been an exhausting day and he was glad when he could call it quits and turn in for the night. He fell asleep promptly and did not awake until his usual time Thursday morning. This surprised him, for he had expected some nocturnal activity. But there had been not a sound, nor had any trap been tampered with. So be it. He would try again that night, perhaps using all seven this time.

When the results were the same Friday morning, even

though he had deployed the sixth trap near to where the bag of hamster food had been destroyed and the seventh on one of the stair landings leading to the playroom, Bart knew he was in over his head. He would have to seek out Cletus Washington.

Clete, as everyone called him, was the superintendent of an apartment building around the corner from Bart's house, and he pursued a lucrative refurbishing business on the side, specializing in refrigerators and air conditioners. Of indeterminate age, Bart estimated him to be in his mid-fifties, judging from the occasional white hair that sprinkled his close-cropped round head. A solid bear of a man, he stood a good six feet.

Clete was an institution in the neighborhood, its sentimental if not duly elected mayor, mother hen, answer man, Rock of Gibraltar. His ways were as mysterious as they were successful, and he could repair anything from broken faucets to shattered spirits. If the spare part was not in his workshop or in himself, he knew precisely where else to look. Whatever the predicament brought him, his expression never changed. It reminded Bart of a Cheshire cat's. But Bart had a hunch that Clete used his manner, his easy humor and ready laugh, to keep people from coming too close, for even though he seemed always to be smiling, his eyes never were.

Clete had been helpful to Bart on several occasions over the years, most recently at the height of the mouse infestation, and Bart credited Clete's advice at the time with having significantly shortened the ordeal. Even so, he had sought him out only occasionally since and disliked having to go to him now.

Bart liked Clete well enough and assumed Clete liked him, yet there was something in Clete that made Bart slightly uneasy whenever he was with him. He had not been able to define it precisely and so had simply kept his distance. Chances were, however, that he would have the kind of information Bart felt he needed and he therefore saw no alternative but to seek Clete's help that evening.

As soon as Bart reached the office, he telephoned Meg to tell her he would not be coming up for the weekend. She was disappointed, but her concern for his safety and well-being on learning there *was* a rat loose in the house far outweighed it.

"Oh, I do wish you'd get an exterminator in there," she pressed him, a clear note of urgency in her voice this time.

"Well, I'm going to see Clete this afternoon, and I'm sure he'll have lots of ideas."

"That's a start, Bart darling, but it seems to me that's not the same. I mean, an exterminator..."

"Sweetheart, I promise," he interrupted her. "If I don't nail this guy over the weekend, I'll get hold of one first thing Monday morning. Really!"

She accepted this, but with a marked lack of enthusiasm.

Bart could not sit still for more than minutes at a stretch the entire day, fabricating one mission after another requiring him to get up and out of his office. To the water cooler and back, then the men's room, down the hall to someone else's office for something, over to his picture window to gaze at the street below, ten floors down. My God, all those people down there. They looked like a swarm of scurrying ants. Or were they mice? Or rats? Finally, it was time to go home and to look for Clete.

As he turned onto Clete's block, he saw him at the other end, lounging on the railing of his stoop and hailing the passing parade of his constituency.

"Hey, there, Clete!" Bart greeted him when he thought he was within earshot.

"Hey, there yourself!" Clete shot back. In all the years they had known each other, Clete had never once called Bart by name. "Where've you been? Long time no see," Clete added a bit petulantly.

"Sorry about that. Been busy as hell. Time got away from me, I guess," Bart sought to mend his fences.

"Here! Pull up a chair!" Clete smiled, once the formalities were over, pointing at the fourth step. He dropped onto it himself. "Ooof!" he exhaled. "Long day. What's up?"

"I think I'm in real trouble, Clete."

"Oh? Sorry to hear that. More mice?"

"No. More like a rat."

"Oh! That's bad."

"I know," Bart agreed, shaking his head ruefully.

"Know anything about them?"

"No more than I read at the library the other day."

"Library?" Clete snorted disdainfully. "Jesus! No book's gonna teach you how to fight a rat...in real life, I mean."

"So I found out."

"What makes you think it's a rat, anyway?"

"I thought it was another mouse at first but then, no matter what I tried I couldn't catch it, and then the damage started to happen..."

"What damage?" he interrupted.

"First the drain hose on the clothes washer, then the telephone line and after that the toaster's electrical cord, but the clincher was when the two guys from the protection company I use showed me the rat droppings..."

"Well, thanks for telling me," he said, starting to rise. "Let me know how you make out."

"Wait a minute, Clete," Bart protested, baffled. "I need your help...badly."

"Don't sound much like it to me...since it seems you already got two guys in the picture," Clete said, his nose plainly out of joint.

"All they did was identify the problem, Clete, and that's a hell of a way from catching the damn thing," Bart explained, reassuring him of his importance, hoping the tempest would pass.

"You bet your sweet ass it is," Clete said, relaxing back, resting his elbows on the fifth step.

"My wife's been after me to get an exterminator. What do you think of that idea?"

"Not much. Exterminators are for old ladies and guys who either got too much dough or are scared of getting their hands dirty. You one of them?"

"That's the way I feel, too, Clete, and that's what I said to her...in effect, anyway."

"First thing you gotta learn about a rat is that he's a survivor. So, while you're spending about twenty-five or thirty percent of your time thinking about him...because you got other things to do besides, of course...he's there spending a hundred percent of his concentrating on you and how he can outsmart you...because that's *all* he's got to think about. So, the first thing you gotta get in your head is just because you're bigger than him don't make you smarter. This is no mouse you're up against now, you understand. Okay?"

"Okay."

"Good. Now, there're five ways to kill a rat, mostly. Traps...that's the most obvious, but sometimes they don't work so good, so you gotta try something else...poisons... and then there's clubbing, or you can gas 'em or shoot 'em."

Bart was tempted to tell Clete he knew most of this

from his research at the library and thereby cut the dialogue short, but he thought better of it.

"Now, in a house like you got, forget about gassing and shooting. Obvious reasons. So, you're gonna have to rely on one of the other three...or, in some cases, all of them. Whatever you can get to work for you."

"I see."

"Now, far as poisons go, there's two main kinds: the one that thins his blood and the one that works with water. That's the kind I like. Less messy."

They had arrived at new ground for Bart and what he had come to hear.

"Less messy?" Bart encouraged him.

"That's right. Other one works on the idea of getting his blood so thin, he hemorrhages. Well, that's okay, so long as he does his bleeding outside, but there's no guarantee he'll do that, and that can sure as hell make some mess out of your house."

"Whew!" Bart grimaced, picturing it.

"So, like I say, I'm partial to the other. That's not saying that you won't have some of the same problem... especially if you got some leaky faucets around...but since it depends on water, he's gotta go out of the house to find it...like out in the sewer."

"You lost me, Clete."

"Okay, let me back up some. What you do first is spread the stuff around all the places you think he's likely to go... that's another problem you got with rats, they're smart, so they're secret. I mean, you'll see his droppings all over the place and the hell he's raising, but by the time you do, he's already hightailed it out of there. Real ... especially in a house where there's so much room to run around in. But, anyhow, so you put the stuff along walls, in corners, under things, places like that. And along comes mister rat and starts putting the stuff away, and being that he's a rat, he eats like a pig, right?" Clete paused to give Bart a chance to savor the humor. "And then, by and by, when he's had his fill, he gets hit with this terrible, powerful thirst. He's just gotta find water. Goes crazy till he does...and you don't want to be anywhere around when he's looking, because if he thinks you're standing in the way, he's likely as not to come after you instead..."

"Jesus!"

"That's right. Anyways, like I say, he'll end up finding it in the sewer outside...unless of course you've been kinda dumb and left some around for him...and soon as he starts drinking, no matter how much he drinks, he can't get enough. That God-awful terrible thirst just won't go away...until finally he goes POOF!"

"Poof?"

"That's right. Blows all to hell. Ever seen a balloon's got too much air in it? Well, in this here case, it's water."

"You mean the rat blows apart...into lots of little pieces? Jesus! That's disgusting!"

"That about sums it up all right. Disgusting. Every frigging thing about them is for that matter. I'd be getting that into my head too, if I was you. But at least when he blows, he's doing it outside and not all over your carpet or your best furniture...if you get my meaning."

"Oh, I get it all right, Clete. But what about toilets? Seems to me if he's looking for water..."

"They can cause a problem, you got a point, especially because rats can swim for three or four days without drowning, you know. I even known them to get into apartments that way. But that don't happen too often. They gotta be awful desperate and sure there's food for them to get at on the other side. But when they have to, they can jump like a frog. So, you ought to keep your toilets closed up."

"You mean literally...shut off?"

"No...lid down, is all. See, it's hard for the rat...I mean, he can still do it, understand...but it's tougher for him to jump and lift a heavy seat at the same time."

"Oh, yes, I see," shaking his head. "Christ! That's hard to believe, Clete...not that I don't, you understand," he quickly corrected himself. "But, I mean, have you known them to come up from the sewer like that...into your toilet?"

"Not to me. But to a friend of mine. Super I know over on Eighty-first. Or anyway, that's what he said..."

"Really?" prompting him.

"Yeah. Told me he went to sit down one morning and there this rat was...swimming around, looking up at him. He saw it just in time, barely did manage to get his ass and everything else that belonged to him out of the way and the lid slammed back down." He laughed. "Poor bastard was still shaking telling me about it. But I guess he finally got rid of it by flushing and flushing until it got tired of being spun around in there and went back to where it come from."

"Oh, Christ, Clete!" Bart moaned.

"Yeah, I know how you feel. Nothing to fool with, but you'll be okay. You just gotta pay attention to what you're doing, not be some smart ass, thinking you got all the answers."

"No chance of that, Clete. Never has been...and even less, after listening to you," he flattered him intentionally. "But, Clete, where do I get some of the stuff you're talking about?"

"I can let you take some of mine. No need of it right at

the moment. Give it to you at cost...plus a little...you know, to cover my expenses, is all."

"That's swell of you, Clete." Bart saw a ray of light at the end of the tunnel for the first time since he sat down.

"But only one thing. I can't guarantee he won't be immune. Some turn out to be. Eat the goddam stuff like it was candy. That can get pretty discouraging if that happens."

"And what if it does to me? Be just my luck."

"Then you gotta try some of the other ways I was telling you about. Maybe go back to the traps. Or clubbing. Which reminds me, there's something else you can do which I forgot to mention in the beginning. It's akin to clubbing...something called blocking."

Bart looked at him quizzically.

"Pretty much like it sounds. Sometimes you get lucky and you can catch the rat coming out its hole. And since rats got no more liking for humans than the other way around, chances are when he sees you, he's gonna shag his ass right back where he come from. And you'll be there, ready to shove your club or whatever you got, bang in there after him. You'll be just like locking his front door on him."

"Oh, come on, Clete! What in hell are my chances of being there when I'm supposed to be?"

"Well, for one thing, rats come out of their hiding places at night looking for food. So that's the best time for blocking and clubbing, too. They don't usually come out in daytime...don't like doing their thing in the light... unless you just happen to stumble on him, scare him into the open."

"To tell the truth, Clete, I'm not that sure how effective I would be in that kind of situation."

"It can scare you, all right, but, like you just said, it's a long shot and I guess that's why I forgot to mention it first off. Anyways, I wouldn't go looking for chances, because clubbing and blocking both can be kind of dangerous. Means you gotta get closer to the rat than most people care to."

"Me, anyway," Bart admitted, smiling weakly. "Besides, most rats don't scare all that easy...specially when they're hungry...which is all the goddam time...and they think you're in the way or they feel like you're threatening them. Then they can be mean as hell...to you personal... scared of nothing, nothing, nothing."

Bart, feeling he was suffocating, sighed deeply.

"I remember," Clete continued, "having to mess with one five or six years ago now ...building up on Ninety-fifth, couple blocks from the river. Nice place, clean. But I got me a hunch one day a rat was out back. Droppings all over the place, a lot of things chewed up. So, I got myself a tarp out of the cellar and laid it across the top of this barrel. But first, I put a chunk of raw meat in there. And then I laid this tarp out, nice and neat. And sure enough, the old gent comes trundling out, his whiskers twitching, screwing up his nose, catching all them sweet smells of that meat, ready for the taking, and up he scampers...just like a fly...right up the side of that wooden barrel..."

"Jesus!"

"That's right. Except you know what happened when he got there?"

"Fell in?"

"That's what I was hoping for. Go for the meat without looking first. But he's too smart for that. Instead of going across the tarp like I wanted him to, this son of a bitch scoots under it...damn near lifts up the edge to get himself a look inside first. Would you believe it?"

Bart shook his head in wonder.

"I should've clubbed him right then and there with the two-by-four I was holding. Would've cut the son of a bitch in half. But I guess I was too interested seeing what he'd do next."

"You mean you were that close to him?"

"Couple feet. That's what I don't like about this clubbing business. Anyway, in he drops like a goddam stone. And then he starts running around down there all over the damn place, and I knew it wouldn't be long before he was on his way up. So, to beat him to the punch, I ripped off the tarp and, sure enough, here he comes holding that piece of meat in his mouth bigger'n he was..."

"And where were you by this time, Clete?"

"Leaning over the barrel, watching him come. And so, I give him a good swat side of the head, and that sent him back down...but you know, the old bastard, he never let go that meat."

"After you hit him square in the face?"

"You know it. And so, while I have him down there, I start to whale the hell out of him...or try to, anyway... poking that two-by-four at him. But he keeps dodging this way and that, running here, there, always managing to get out of the way. No matter how I tried, I just couldn't nail him, and I knew by then if I didn't nail his ass and damn quick, he was gonna nail mine."

"Weren't you scared?"

"You bet your sweet ass I was scared. I never come up against anything like this guy before...smart...tough. Anyway, I keep taking my licks at him, hoping I'd connect in time, but then one of these times, the son of a bitch grabs hold of the end of that two-by-four I was using and starts coming after me...right up the goddam shaft. I knew then he was coming for my eyes. Rats'll do that, you know...go for the softest body parts first—like the eyes—

best way for the rat to get at the brain. Anyway, I knew this was what the rat had in mind for mine and that my time was running out. I guess you could say I was getting desperate, not too sure I was gonna get out of this one."

"I can believe it." Bart shuddered.

"I took that two-by-four and started swinging it and waving it every which way, round and round, up and down, trying my damnedest to shake the old codger loose. But he just kept holding on for all he was worth. I thought sure my arms would give out. It was a tossup, him or me, who'd have to give in first. And just when I was about to, he let go. And he went flying through the air BAM! up against the wall."

Clete clapped his hands for emphasis. It caught Bart by surprise and made him jump.

"The way he hit that wall," Clete went on, oblivious, "the goddam force of it, I was sure he was done for. But, no, not this one. He just gets up, shakes himself off once or twice, figures out where in hell he's at, and takes off for his hole, disappearing into it in nothing flat. Never seen the likes of it."

Neither said anything for quite a spell after Clete had completed his yarn, each locked in thought. Then, abruptly, both started to speak at once.

"No, you go ahead, Clete," Bart said, deferring to him.

"Well, I was just gonna say, you had to admire the old guy."

"I suppose," Bart agreed.

"Anyway, now I told you everything I know," Clete said, with a don't-you-believe-it glint in his eye. He dug out the large box of poison he had promised Bart and handed it to him. "I'll figure how much and let you know, okay?"

"Sure, swell...but did you?"

"What's that?"

"Catch him?"

"Oh, that...Of *course!*" he replied defiantly, as if stunned that any such question could be asked. "Just took me a couple extra days, is all."

Bart felt ashen, inside and out.

"Well," Clete said, rising abruptly after another silence "the wife's waiting on me for supper and sure to be wondering by now what's happened to me. But you welcome to stay on, if you care to."

"Thanks, Clete, I think I'll take you up on that...for a little while, anyway," Bart replied. He needed time to gather and straighten his thoughts.

More to the point, he was in no great hurry to reach home and what he knew awaited him there.

Six

"Sooner or later, goddammit!" Bart exhorted himself aloud, clasping his hands to his knees and getting up. He had lingered on Clete's stoop far in excess of the "little while" he had told him he would. The street lights had started to flicker on. Time was running out.

He set forth with forced resolve, turned right at the avenue, right again onto his block, and there it was. It seemed to be standing apart from those around it, even though it was almost impossible to tell where one house began and the other ended.

Ever since discovering that he had to contend with a rat and not a mouse, Bart's greatest concern was accidentally triggering a direct confrontation, and this was what was at the back of his mind the past several days as he entered his house. He had no sure way of ascertaining the rat's whereabouts, how far it might have wandered from its home base and how endangered it would feel as a consequence.

Bart's hope remained to deal with the rat at arm's length, relying on the traps, and now the poison, to do the job. He had absolutely no desire for hand-to-hand combat.

And so, that evening he put into effect his first policy decision, still fresh from formulation while he sat on Clete's stoop.

First, he made a great racket at the front door, so that there could be no mistaking his arrival.

Second, he did nothing hurriedly, no abrupt, unexpected moves, nothing alarming, once he had opened the door.

Third, he waited under the stoop a solid minute or more to give the rat ample time to regain its sanctuary.

Bart was so satisfied with the results that he decided to make this standard procedure for the duration.

The second decision made while on Clete's stoop was to restrict use of the poison to the kitchen for two reasons. In light of its past success at finding ample food there, the rat was certain to continue to look to the kitchen as a major source. Secondly, Bart wanted to remember exactly where it was distributed. A forgotten cache somewhere in the house for the family's dog to get into later would be unforgivable.

Bart poured the poison generously along three of the room's four walls, concentrating it behind the floor cabinets, the refrigerator and the stove, as far as he could hurl it from the carton. It did not stretch as much as he would have liked, but it was a solid start, and Clete had promised him more if he needed it.

After collecting the seven traps, replacing the bait and redistributing them more or less as before, Bart felt he had earned his nightly scotch on the rocks. Because it was Friday, he allowed himself a second and then headed around the corner to a steak house where the fare was plain but wholesome and the service fast. He was glad to return home. It had been another long day. Bart went directly upstairs hoping he would be able to sleep.

As he passed the linen closet on the third floor, Bart thought he heard a small commotion coming from behind the closed door. He wanted to dismiss it as nothing, as his imagination combining with the stillness in the empty house to play tricks on him. But was it? He pressed his ear to the door and impulsively grabbed the knob.

Not a large room, the closet, lined with shelves from floor to ceiling, nevertheless served as the central depot for the entire house. It was also the repository for sundry small belongings not yet ready for storage in the cellar.

The suction tugging against the opening door pulled a swirl of tiny white feathers into the hallway where he stood and roiled those already blanketing the floor. A fresh supply cascaded from the top shelf, fluttered down, their flat sides catching the ceiling light as if they had been wafting tinsel.

Every shelf was in disarray. Several dress shirts, seldom used, still snug in their paper-and-cellophane wrappers from the laundry, had been shoved from one shelf and lay sprawled below. Towels and wool blankets, sheets and pillow cases, once neatly stacked, looked more like they had been thrown there by someone standing in the hall.

Bart reached high for the offending pillow, taking pains to avoid unleashing another downpour. He inched it toward him. A few feathers managed to break loose and float earthward. From where he stood, he could see the ragged hole that had been torn into its side.

Suddenly, there was a frantic scratching and scurrying along the top shelf. Bart stopped everything, including his breathing, and waited, his eyes fastened upward. A dull thud. Movement in a child's suitcase, jammed into the deepest corner. He sprang for it, hauling it off the shelf with his full might, slamming it to the floor. A thick cloud of tiny white feathers exploded all around it at impact.

Clete had said nothing about stomping, but stomping it would be and stomping it was. Again and again, he slammed his foot down on the plywood suitcase. Its sides collapsed. Again. Again. He had become crazed, as if possessed. Again. Again. Finally, the pain shooting into his calf became too much for him. He had to quit.

Bart staggered backward, his legs rubbery, coming to rest against the banister in the hallway, out of breath, sweating, wild-eyed, his arms limp at his side.

"Jesus!" he said softly, staring down at the suitcase. It was in ruins. But there was not a sign of life from within, not a sound. "Jesus!" he said again, almost in a sigh, tottering to his bedroom and shutting the door behind him.

He fell onto his bed and into a deep sleep. Within an hour, he was awake, uncertain where he was and why he was still fully dressed, his mind racing between fact and fiction as to what had actually happened. Waves of temptation swept over him to return to the scene, but none strong enough to compel him to do it. He undressed, tried to sleep, but it was early dawn before finally he succeeded.

The birds chirping outside his window and brilliant sunshine awoke him. He looked at the clock on his bedside table. He had overslept, would be late for work. Damn! Then, he realized it was Saturday, and, oh yes, he remembered, there was the linen closet and what was in it to deal with.

Bart cautiously opened his bedroom door and peered into the hallway. All was still, all was clear. Guardedly, he approached the closet, reached through the open door and felt for the overhead light. The place was in chaos, clothes lying about, linen strewn helter-skelter, and the suitcase, smashed and vanquished, lying in its bed of tiny white feathers.

With his weight on his right leg, and holding onto the door as best he could for support, he stretched for the suitcase with the tip of his bare big toe. Closer. Closer. There! Gradually, bit by bit, he raised the shattered, wobbly lid.

Suddenly, the door gave, swaying out from under him. He teetered, lost his balance, reeled backward. The lid dropped shut.

"You son of a bitch!" Bart cursed, recovering, and violently kicked the lid off.

Bart gaped in disbelief as an icy surge of uncertainty swept over him. The suitcase was empty.

It required the better part of an hour to straighten the shelves, gather the darting elusive little feathers, and vacuum the place clean. Throughout, Bart kept thinking he would come across some evidence of the rat having been there, but there was none, not even a few droppings. Nor could he figure out how it had gained access to the suitcase, short of having lifted the lid itself. But how could that be? Though flattened, its latches were still in the locked position. Again, that chill of uncertainty.

Hopefully, he sought affirmation one way or the other from the traps or the poison. But there was none. Neither had been disturbed during the night.

Although he had not planned on it, immediately he set out to find Clete. He was in his workshop.

"Well! How'd you make out?" Clete greeted him.

"Not too well, I'm afraid."

"That's too bad. How come?"

"Eight traps and all the poison you gave me and nothing."

"Can't blame me."

"I'm not *blaming* anyone, Clete. I'm just reporting to you what happened, that's all."

"What bait did you use?"

"Sharpest cheddar cheese I could lay my hands on."

"That wasn't too smart."

Bart didn't know what he had said or done to get himself into an adversary position with Clete.

"I didn't know what else to..."

"Rats are onto cheese. People been using it so long on traps, rats think twice soon as they come across it. Can smell danger."

"Really? And what about the poison?"

"I told you. Maybe your guy's on to that, too. And maybe he's starting to nibble at it, slow and cautious like, without you knowing anything about it."

"But I thought you told me once they started, they couldn't stop with that stuff."

"That's just what I'm saying to you. Maybe he's trying it out...to see if a little does him any harm...then, if he sees it don't, he'll go after it big."

"Whew! That's pretty sophisticated."

"If that's another way of saying that they're smart, you're right."

"So, Clete, if the cheese is no good..." Bart sought to cool the conversation.

"You use bacon...raw bacon strips."

"I never heard of that," Bart blurted, instantaneously regretting it.

"That so?" icily. "Well, you have now."

"Okay, Clete. I'll get some right away."

"You gotta be sure and tie the bacon on good and tight. Make the son of a bitch tug to get it off. Better his chances of getting caught, you know?"

Although the conversation was far less pleasant than

their previous one, Bart felt he was gaining far more useful information.

"Okay, fine, Clete. This is really helpful."

"See what happens," Clete said, returning to the refrigerator motor he had been working on when Bart had interrupted him.

Bart wanted to keep the consultation alive, but clearly it was over.

"Okay, thanks, Clete. I'll keep you posted."

"You do that little thing," Clete said. Bart started for home.

"Hey!" Clete called after him when he was fifteen or twenty feet away. "What about the rubber gloves?"

"Ru...rubber gloves? What...?"

"Yeah. Like I told you yesterday. Did you use rubber gloves when you went to baiting?"

"You didn't..." Bart began, decided not to press.

"Could be the rat picked up human smells off the traps, and if he did, no way he was gonna touch 'em."

"I didn't know that."

"What do you mean you didn't know that? Weren't you listening? Like I was telling you. Rats got that special sense in them, tells them where danger is in plenty of time, so they can avoid it...keeps them from getting hurt. So, if they can smell your hands on the traps, they'll know goddam well that spells nothing but trouble and they'll stay away...no matter what you try and do to get them to go for it. Tonight, when you go to baiting, wash the traps good and then use gloves. Okay?"

"You're on."

"You know, I seen them starve themselves to death, right next to a trap that's got the bait still on it, or next to a pile of food they suspect is got poison in it. Amazing thing. But from now on, I can't help you none unless you listen to what I'm saying to you."

The unfairness of the accusation made Bart smart, but he held his tongue as he continued home. He detoured by the delicatessen for a package of bacon. On the way to the checkout counter, he spotted a pair of rubber gloves and picked these up, too.

"Family all away, Mr. Hughes?" the proprietor asked, totaling Bart's purchases.

"Yes. Maine."

"That must be nice for them."

"I try to get up there every weekend I can."

"Can't say I blame you," the man said. "Say, I hope you don't mind me saying so, but you look like you could use a little vacation up there yourself."

"I got away for the Fourth, but since then, I've been dealing with this goddam rat that got into my house. Don't want to leave until I nail the S.O.B."

"They can be bad news, all right. What are you using to do the job?"

"Traps mostly. And poison, naturally." He was reminded that he had forgotten to get more from Clete and made a mental note to double back before going home.

"Tried any of this?" the man asked, handing Bart a box he'd removed from the shelf.

"I'm using stuff Cletus Washington gave me...you know, Clete?"

"Sure, I know him. 'Gave you,' you say? That doesn't sound much like the Cletus Washington I know," he laughed.

"Yes, well, 'sold' *would* perhaps be more accurate," Bart joined in. "Anyway, it's supposed to work with water. Clete claims it's better than the other stuff."

"That so? I'd say the exact opposite, myself. Tried them all out in the country. Don't get too much call for it around these parts, of course."

Bart noticed for the first time the descriptive material on the side of the box. It spoke in elaborate terms of the quick demise of victims through hemorrhaging.

"Why don't you play it safe...give the guy a choice?" the proprietor suggested with a twinkle in his eye.

"What can I lose?" Bart agreed, departing, just as glad there was no need to return to Cletus for now.

He dropped off his purchases at the house, grabbed his briefcase from the dining room table and spent the afternoon in Central Park, working his way through it. The day was made to order for it. Besides, he welcomed the excuse to be out of the house.

That evening, he soaked the traps in boiling water to wash off those "human smells" Clete had talked about, and scrubbed them with a bristle brush afterward for good measure. Donning his cumbersome rubber gloves, he dried them and began the loading process. The more he worked with the bacon, the more it softened into a pulpy, greasy mass, slithering between his fingers and rendering the string slippery and uncooperative. More than once, the knot closed on the tip of his gloves. But he stuck to it and eventually completed the job.

As far as he could tell, he had done it to perfection, following Clete's advice to the letter. He spread the new poison, being careful not to mix it with the old, just in case the rat was testing it as Clete had suggested. Any change, even the smallest, could alert the rat to danger, cause it to quit.

This was his best effort. He was sure of it.

But Sunday brought him yet another failure.

"Christ Almighty! What *more* do you want?" he yelled

out angrily at the rat, loudly enough to be heard wherever it was lurking.

Bart wanted to run for Clete, but he didn't. Even though he had obtained useful new information from him, it had been a mistake going to him yesterday, so soon after their first go-around. Clete's testiness had been proof of that. Bart had no wish to wear out his welcome and risk losing Clete as his backstop altogether. Besides, there was always tomorrow.

It wasn't that Bart was immune to discouragement, only that he refused to yield to it without a fight...too stubborn for that. Of course, it was disconcerting, not to mention very worrisome, having to share his home with an uninvited visitor. But it had happened to him before, after all, or something closely approximating it anyway, and he had persevered against it, carrying the day in the end. Why not again?

Meg called shortly after he had completed his nightly ritual and was just putting his rubber gloves back in the cabinet under the sink.

"We all missed you terribly," she said. "The weekend was just endless without you here."

"Same for me," he said, meaning it.

"How's it going?" she asked, a tentativeness in her voice.

"You mean with the rat?"

"Yes."

"Nothing so far."

"Oh, I was afraid you'd say that. So that means you'll be getting hold of the exterminator tomorrow as you said?"

Bart did not answer.

"Bart?" her voice rising. "Bart, you will get hold of an

exterminator tomorrow, won't you?" she pressed, betraying her concern.

"Sure." he agreed, to placate her. "I said I would, didn't I?"

"Oh, thank God! I was so afraid you might have changed your mind about it. Every time I think of you locked in that house alone with that awful rat, it makes me positively sick. I even wake up at night thinking about it."

"It's not so bad. Sounds worse than it is. Frustrating more than anything else," he said, hoping this would reassure her.

"Well, I'll breathe a lot easier after that exterminator has been there, I'll tell you that."

Bart did not call the exterminator Monday morning. How could he and still keep Clete in the picture? He was bound to get wind of it and that would be that. Besides, Bart was doing all that was humanly possible to catch the rat. What more could an exterminator do? Time was what was needed. Time and patience and persistence.

He tried the traps with bacon *and* cheese. And waited. He tried some with peanut butter, others without, and waited some more. He tried them inundated with honey. He tried pouring rich doses of granulated sugar over both poisons he had spread so liberally, convinced by now that the rat was not into either as he had so fervently been hoping. He tried the traps where he thought the rat would not go, since he was having so little luck placing them where he thought it would.

Nothing, absolutely nothing, no variant, no combination, no location caught the rat's fancy.

By Thursday morning, he was at his wits' end and knew, whatever the consequences, he must go back to Clete, and right away.

"Sure thought I would've heard from you before

now," Clete said hardly looking up from the air conditioner he was working on.

"I wish I had something good to tell you, Clete, but I've struck out every time."

"You mean you haven't caught him yet?"

"That's just what I mean. I've done everything, just as you told me...gloves, bacon, tying it on, peanut butter... every goddam thing, and nothing has worked. Nothing."

"And what's the rat been up to all this time?"

"Beats the hell out of me, Clete. I haven't heard a sound out of him since I saw you last Saturday."

"You sure you *got* a rat?" Clete reacted brusquely, adding, not without a touch of cruelty, "I mean besides the one that's rattling around inside your head." Bart looked down at the ground. "I don't know," he said meekly. "I'm not sure of anything anymore." He sounded defeated.

"Well, it sure as hell doesn't make all that much sense to me, having all this trouble and taking all this time, I'll tell you that. Anyway. You been putting the traps where he's got his nest...like I told you?"

Bart could have argued the point of what Clete had or had not told him, but recognized the futility of it.

A curious expression had crossed Clete's face. Had he not known better, Bart would have sworn that he was deriving some sort of sadistic pleasure from his terrible plight.

"I don't *know* where the goddam nest is, Clete," Bart said wearily. "How in *hell* am I supposed to know *that?*"

"You got a cellar?" His tone was harsh.

"Of course," Bart answered defensively.

"Well?"

"Well, what?" Bart was starting to get angry.

"You looked down there?" Clete asked tartly.

Damn this man, Bart thought, controlled himself, said only, "No. No, I haven't, Clete."

"Well, *that* ain't so goddam smart. How in hell you expect to catch the son of a bitch not knowing where the damn thing lives...where to put all your efforts?"

"I guess the truth of it is, Clete," Bart confessed, "I've sort of been hoping there'd be another way...that it'd go for the traps or the poison...so that I wouldn't have to go down there and risk running into him and getting into an all-out fight right there...just the two of us...you know?"

"Of *course*, I know! Who the hell wouldn't? But maybe you're not gonna be that lucky. From what you say, sounds to me like it's already too late for the traps. The guy's onto them. You should've thought of that last week when you first found out what you had."

"But why didn't you say some--?"

"I figured a smart feller like you'd know *that* much," Clete interrupted sarcastically. "But anyhow, looks to me now, if you want him, you're gonna have to go down there and get him. You've got no choice."

"Jesus!" Bart shuddered at the prospect. "I'm not sure I can do that."

"You know," Clete said, fixing Bart with his steady gaze, "sometimes in life, comes a time when people gotta get their hands dirty," adding after, a deliberate pause, "even for the book kind like you."

This was not what Bart had meant at all, but had Clete hurled a bucket of ice water into his face, he could not have been more shocked at this stunning revelation of his true sentiments about him. He noted that the look of contented cat had been replaced by a storm cloud and that Clete's eyes were cold and resentful.

Whatever the root cause of Clete's rancor, Bart was certain he was the brunt, not the source, but it was equally clear to him that his days of being able to rely on him for companionship and direction were at an end.

There was nothing left for him to do but to extricate himself with as much grace as he could muster and with what little dignity he had left. Clete did not seem the least mindful, having returned to the piece of machinery he had on his workbench.

"Thanks for all your help, Clete," Bart said, meaning it.

Clete's subsequent wave was more a gesture of dismissal than acknowledgment.

That evening, on his return from work, Bart studiously avoided looking in Clete's direction when he walked past his building. The passage of an entire day had failed to take the edge off either his hurt or his anger.

The instant he set foot in the kitchen, he noticed it. A reddish-brown substance had trickled from the cupboard over the stove, down the polished aluminum hood and onto the stove itself. Bart recognized it immediately as dried blood. The rat had gotten into the anticoagulant poison Bart had bought at the delicatessen, just as the proprietor had assured him it would. Bart knew the rat was in that cupboard, dead.

The elation he should have felt was overshadowed by the prospect of now having to clean up the gore. Bart felt queasy and reluctant.

Nevertheless, he overcame his revulsion and purposefully strode toward the death scene. Without permitting himself to break stride, he flung open the double doors. A torrent of thick fluid which had been dammed behind burst forth, cascading down the aluminum hood and splashed onto the stove below.

A family-size ketchup bottle inside the cupboard shifted and rolled into a new position. And covering the shelf itself were dried reddish-brown footprints in dozens of interlocking patterns.

Bart recoiled in horror.

Gradually, he regained his composure and turned to the supply cabinet under the stainless-steel double sink for what he would need to clean up the mess. The inside was in shambles.

Boxes of powdered detergent had been knocked over, their contents spilled everywhere. Packages of soap had been ripped open, the bars themselves lacerated into shreds. The plastic water bucket had been gnawed into uselessness, as had packets of new sponges.

And, as for the rubber gloves Bart had been using, these had been ripped into pieces, as though having been attacked in a frenzy of revenge.

SEVEN

CLETE WAS RIGHT, of course, damn him. The twilight war was over. And Bart knew he had to take the battle the next step, downstairs, into the cellar.

He would attack with the first light of day.

But before then, he would have to telephone Meg to alert her to the possibility of his not being able to make it for the third consecutive weekend. He wasn't looking forward to that either, but made the call that night.

"Oh, Bart, no," she objected, her tone more disappointed than angry. "Janet and Bill Fharquar are expecting us for dinner tomorrow night. They asked us weeks ago."

"I know what a disappointment it is for you, Meg, darling, and believe me, it's a hell of a one for me, too."

"But..."

"It's just that now...after this long process of elimination...I've finally been able to pinpoint where he actually is," Bart explained gently, "and this gives me my first real shot at nailing him."

"But what does the exterminator say?"

Bart had been expecting it and knew what he would do if the subject came up.

"He thinks the way I do, Meg, that it'd be a real pity to let up now...now that we've got him cornered."

"Oh, I see," she said resignedly.

"He also said," Bart embellished, seeing how well his lie had been accepted, "that there's no telling how much more hell the rat could raise with each passing day, so that time is a really compelling factor."

"Oh, darn," she said adding after a pause, "still, I was the one who persuaded you to get him to come, so I guess I have no choice but to go along with what he recommends."

"Apologize to the Fharquars for me, will you, Meg, darling? I really *am* sorry."

"I know you are, Bart. It's not your fault. Just rotten luck, is all. I'm just glad you don't have to fight that thing by yourself...that that exterminator is right there with you."

"I know. Me, too," he said softly.

Bart had never lied to Meg and hated having to do so now, but what else could he do under the circumstances? If she knew that he had not called the exterminator, she would be furious. If she thought he was taking on the rat all by himself, she would be worried to death. No, he had done the right thing.

He set the alarm for an hour earlier than usual to allow time to reconnoiter the cellar thoroughly before having to leave for work, and thereby give himself a full day to draw up his battle plans.

In fact, he beat the buzzer by several minutes and bounded eagerly out of bed. He was looking forward to recapturing the initiative, to getting off the receiving end. But as the moment neared, he grew less and less enthusiastic. As so often happens, the decision was proving easier to make than to carry out.

Bart put the kettle to boil and reached into the top half of the bread container for a pair of English muffins. The package of muffins collapsed before his advancing fingers. Instinctively, he yanked his hand out. The lid clanked shut noisily. Bart's breath had accelerated. He stared suspiciously at the container.

He waited a moment, biting his lower lip nervously, and then cautiously took hold of the bottom right corner of the lid, using only the tip of his index finger, and slowly lifted it. As the opening widened, he peered deeper and deeper into the shelf.

"I thought so!" he exploded.

The package had been burrowed into, and not a remnant remained of the muffins it once protected. Hesitantly, Bart raised the lower lid. As he feared, the rat had been into this tier also, leaving the loaf of bread it housed with a large, deep lesion and the shelf itself covered with rat droppings.

"Oh, God! You filthy son of a bitch!" Bart shuddered aloud in disgust, shaking the crumbs and the droppings and what was left of the paper packages into the plastic waste bin next to the stove. He was tempted to throw in the container after them, but decided to wait.

The kettle started to whistle. Grateful for the diversion, he poured the steaming water over the instant-coffee crystals at the bottom of his cup. Maybe something warm would help.

He reached for the box of granulated sugar from the food-supply cabinet. Hardly had it cleared the shelf than its contents started streaming onto the floor through the large, jagged hole opened in its backside. Bart dropped the box as though it had been on fire.

In a silent rage, he began to explore other parts of the cabinet.

One by one, he removed the boxes of food stowed there. One by one, he discovered they had been similarly invaded. Twenty-three boxes and cartons and paper bags in all. None completely consumed, every one effectively and deliberately contaminated.

It took him over an hour to clear up the damage, filling and refilling the plastic waste bin, and dumping it into the garbage cans outdoors. When he had finished, all that remained of his formerly lush food stock was a half-bottle of instant coffee, a little half-and-half, and three or four cans of soup for himself, plus the bacon, cheddar cheese and two-thirds-full jar of peanut butter for the rat.

This was it, in its entirety. What he had been forced to throw out must have approached the forty-to-fifty-dollar range, not counting the metal bread box which he decided to toss in at the last minute.

But Bart had too many other, more important things to worry about than to brood over the loss. His earlier resolve to reconnoiter the cellar had been arrived at none too soon, and these more recent discoveries had only served to reinforce it.

He recovered the seven traps, disarmed them and put them to soak in the sink which he had filled with piping hot water, topped with what was left in the kettle. With these sundry chores behind him, he was free to give his full attention to the serious business ahead of him.

Bart suffered no illusions as to just how dangerous it could be for him, once he and the rat were alone, face to face, confined to the relatively small area of the cellar, and he had every intention of equipping himself accordingly.

On his rounds to collect the traps, he had paused in the living room to choose the weapon he planned on taking with him, settling on the iron fireplace poker. He also brought along the flashlight

His biggest concern was in being jumped by the rat, and he was determined to protect himself in this eventuality. He wanted his battle gear, therefore, to cover as much of his body as possible, to be sufficiently thick to offer some defense against claws and teeth, and yet, light enough to be tolerable in an airless cellar.

He found everything he needed in a large wooden chest kept in the downstairs closet and filled with winter clothes: a pair of high-lacing hunting boots, thick corduroy trousers, heavy wool shirt, gloves, and a beige pith helmet which he had inherited from his father, the souvenir of an African safari. He also found a wool ski mask and was tempted by it, rejecting it in the end as being too hot and offering too little real protection in any event.

Outfitted, Bart took a last gulp of coffee, draining the cup, pulled on his gloves and tapped the pith helmet securely onto his head. He picked up the fireplace poker, then the flashlight, remembered about the batteries, wished he had bought fresh ones. Too bad. Would have to do, for now. He was ready.

Originally, the basement had been one vast open space, stretching the length of the building. When Meg and Bart were having the house renovated, however, they decided to split off the front half and make it into a finished playroom. The back half they had left as it was, referring to it afterward always as the cellar, to differentiate it from its neighbor. A heavy steel fire door separated the two.

The cellar's intended purpose had been to house the central heating system, furnace, and hot water tanks. But the renovating contractor, before he had quit the premises, had already corrupted this intent by leaving behind old doors and floor planking, a discarded window frame or two, surplus rolls of fiberglass insulating material, half-empty paint cans and just about anything else he didn't feel like toting away at his expense. And so, it was only natural that it also became the repository of outgrown family treasures no one wanted any longer but didn't have the resolve to discard altogether.

It was an ideal site for any rat on the lookout for a home.

Bart did not like going into the cellar and avoided it as much as possible. He liked it even less now, and his slowing pace, as he neared the playroom floor, showed it. Several times, he was tempted to turn back, but he pushed on defiantly. His mind was made up. The barn-red fire door guarding the cellar looked hostile to him, as though it had decided to cast its lot with the rat and not him. It was always hard to open, requiring some hip action to jar it free. City fire laws, according to the renovating contractor, called for the door being kept closed at all times. True or not, he had hung it slightly askew which assured it even in the event of human failure.

With the moment of truth upon him, he felt less heroic than he had upstairs, equipping himself for battle, and more like a condemned man facing the stake to which he would be tied. He could still turn back. Oh, Jesus, how he would have welcomed the excuse!

He planted his feet in front of the door, reached for the knob, turned it, shut his eyes, filled his lungs and, with a diversionary, piercing bellow, slammed his hip into it. The door flew open at tremendous velocity, breaking his grip on the knob, crashing into the side wall. Scorching, dead air smashed him in the face and sent him reeling backward, gasping, blinking. The cellar was dense black with only the pale triangle of sickly light falling in from the playroom to illuminate it.

Bart stayed put for a few moments, recovering and working out the best approach for accomplishing what he had come to do. So blatantly was he silhouetted in the doorway, the rat could easily have assumed that he was trying to provoke him into attack then and there, and it surely occurred to Bart that he might do just that. But the rat was too experienced and wily to reveal his whereabouts so cheaply. Besides, the conditions weren't right for battle. Bart had too much running room behind him to escape into.

The single electric fixture for the room was a white ceramic socket in the middle of the ceiling. A long string hung from it and a naked bulb was screwed into it. Resolutely, Bart made for it, carefully assuring beforehand the safety of each next step with his flashlight. The rat's hideous radiation permeated the atmosphere. Bart knew he was watching him from somewhere, his silently sliding eyes monitoring his progress, hidden under or behind something, waiting. The accumulated grit of years crackled underfoot and echoed off the stone walls. The only other sound was the pounding in Bart's head.

Suddenly, from behind, came a dull, pronounced thump. Bart wheeled in its direction, wildly spraying the flashlights' narrow beam every which way. "Jesus God! Here he comes!" Maybe there was yet chance of escape, if he could just hide behind the light long enough, use it to distract him, perhaps cause him to break his charge. But where was he? Coming in from behind? From the side? Which side? Bart couldn't find him. Oh, God!

He sprang for the string dangling from the ceiling fixture. It bobbed away, dancing, twirling, evading his grasp infuriatingly. Finally, in one last desperate effort, he caught it, gave it a fearsome tug. The light that came on was pathetic, woefully inadequate for the amount of space it was there to service. It gave off an eerie incandescence, enlarging the shadows created by it, rendering them forbidding, suggestive, hostile. The air was thick with choking, swirling clouds of black dust. Bart was wheezing badly. The rat was nowhere to be seen.

Then he remembered about the fire door. In his obsession with the rat on entering, Bart had neglected to tie the door open with the string attached to the inside knob for that purpose. It had swung shut of its own volition, exactly as it had been designed to do. "Christ!"

Without delay, he retraced his footsteps, gave the door a forceful pull and tied it back. Gratefully, he breathed in the different if not altogether fresh air from the playroom.

Upon reentering the cellar, he noticed a peculiar kind of squeaking, small but insistent. He was positive it had not been there previously. What it was, or where it might be coming from, whether indoors or out, eluded him. He thought of a nest of twittering baby birds.

A cursory glance about the room and it was obvious to Bart that, short of dumb luck, he would never succeed in locating precisely where the rat made his home. Piles of this and that had been abandoned everywhere, as if no one had ever wanted to linger there longer than necessary to make the delivery. Only a thin path had been left clear to reach the furnace and hot-water tanks.

Hence the most Bart could hope for was to establish some sort of *modus operandi* for the rat, where he went, how he got there, what he did. Equipped with this basic information, Bart would then be in a position to place the traps and poison along major travel arteries, perhaps even at the mouths of likely hiding places.

The dust his slightest movement activated made the task arduous in the extreme. Not only did it further dilute the already meager lighting, but it also caused him acute physical discomfort, clogging his lungs, blurring his vision, and turning his sweaty face as black as that of any chimney sweep.

Bart's point of departure was the drain basin for the clothes washer upstairs. It had turned a tattletale gray, and the long neoprene hose the plumber had fitted to the washer itself and fed through the hole in the floor hung awkwardly and stiffly into it. The severed body of its predecessor lay coiled on the bottom like a languishing black snake.

Light from upstairs showed through the hole, disclosing how unnecessarily large it was in relation to the hose it had been cut to accommodate. Clearly, Bart belatedly understood now, this had been the rat's passageway to freedom the night of his arrival. Perhaps he was exploiting it still. Damn the idiot who had made it!

Bart kept moving briskly, while giving himself plenty of time to scour the room as thoroughly as conditions would permit, beaming his flashlight under, behind and into everything he could. He uncovered sufficient rat droppings along the base of foundation walls to be convinced these were significant communication routs, deserving heavy concentration of both traps and poison. Occasionally, he would interrupt his rounds to listen for any signs of life, but the rat maintained his secretiveness and his distance. The cluttering had also ceased.

The flashlight swept over the dollhouse Bart had built for his daughters, Peggy and Evie. The indirect light coming out its windows made it look as if there were life on the inside, someone going from room to room, carrying a flickering candle. Not entirely facetiously, Bart thought he might leave a little poison at the front door at the appropriate time. He pressed ahead.

At first, he didn't know what to make of it. It could

have passed for an ordinary floor drain without its perforated cover. But its location was bizarre for it to be that, off to one side of the room, at the bottom of a deep, rectangular recess. Whatever it was, though, Bart suspected it had no business being open and, when leaning over it for a better look, all uncertainty was erased. The light reflected off a greenish, torpid liquid about three or four inches down the pipe, and the odor rising from it made its connection to or with an active sewer system indisputable.

Bart hadn't the foggiest notion why it had been left that way, much less when or by whom, but it unsettled him to think of the rat being able to commute regularly between his home with him and the entire New York City sewer network.

Bart found the cap deeply imbedded in solidified grime and managed to knock it loose with the fireplace poker. He noticed it had threads around its outer edge and began attempting to engage these with those matching inside the pipe. Both were encrusted with rust and dirt and obstinately refused to take hold.

For better leverage, Bart got down on one knee, using his left hand for support. His head was almost as low as the recess itself, and he was having to hold his breath to avoid inhaling the vile, noxious fumes. The glove on his right hand made working difficult, cumbersome. Impatiently, he wrenched it off and went back to trying to mate the cap and the pipe.

All of a sudden, the squeaking he had initially thought could be a nest of chattering baby birds, resumed, this time louder and more persistent than ever. The sound was so near. Guardedly, he put the cap down, picked up the flashlight and aimed it under the furnace next to him.

Was it only his imagination, conspiring with the alien environment in the cellar, up to its old tricks? He thrust the flashlight deeper into the blackness, his face following close behind, eyes narrowed, searching.

No, it was more than that. There *was* movement back there, undulating, squirming, in the farthest comer.

Using the tip of the poker, Bart stretched for the mass, broke off a small segment and maneuvered it into the open, where he could examine it more closely. He shone the flashlight directly onto it. Even though he had not seen the like before, instinctively he knew what it was.

Bart had uncovered the rat's litter. My God! It had never crossed his mind that he could be a she.

The little body was pink, naked except for a greyish stubble, and its eyes were mere slits. The rest of its features were essentially indistinguishable. It kept trying to get away, to rejoin its brothers and sisters which were, by this time, sending up a sustained clamor of protest.

"Oh, no, you don't," Bart told his captive, holding it fast by the tail with the poker. It wriggled and contorted, putting up a fierce struggle, its tiny feet spinning frantically in a useless effort to gain traction.

Bart was growing increasingly edgy as to the whereabouts of the mother. She was not with them, but surely she could not be far off. This meant time was running against him.

Without further delay, he swept the baby rat toward the rectangular recess and into the yawning pipe. As it hit water level, a faint splash echoed up through and out the hole. Feeling the urgency to get done, Bart sought to shorten the process, dropping the poker and preparing to scoop the rest of the litter to their watery graves with his hand, in one motion.

But his better sense reasserted itself in time. His hand was bare, and it came back to him now in a rush, the story he had once read in a magazine of a young fisherman who had mistaken a nest of baby copperheads for the worms he needed. They must have looked innocent enough to him also, but it had required the next several weeks in hospital for him to recover from their bites. Bart jerked his hand away.

Regloved, he brought the baby rats forward with the poker one by one. They felt soft and mushy, but were far too small to put up more than token resistance. Arriving at the lip of the hole, Bart raised the poker, took careful aim and delivered a sharp rap to the head of each of them, before shoving their lifeless bodies into it.

All but two or three had thus been done in when he heard the creak. Bart rationalized it as something in a pile of renovation material shifting position, readjusting itself as a result of all his moving about. He went for his next victim. Another creak.

Bart's position made him dangerously vulnerable. He was teetering like a tripod with one leg shorter than the others. His head was at knee level, almost resting on the floor. His back was turned.

No longer in doubt, he sprang to his feet and whirled in the direction of the sound. The blood drained from his head; he thought he might faint and fought to regain equilibrium.

The flashlight's beam caught her square in the face and made her beady black eyes blaze wildly. She had him in her sights and was aiming for him in a beeline.

"Yi-a-a-a! Yi-a-a-a!" he screamed, waving the flashlight at her as well, hoping that one or the other or both might succeed in diverting her. But she kept coming at full tilt, as true and undeviatingly as a torpedo traveling just beneath the surface. "Yi-a-a-a! Yi-a-a-a!"

Bart wanted to get ready to smash her with the iron fireplace poker, but he was virtually cornered. He had no room in which to operate, not enough certainly to execute the kind of roundhouse he would need to finish her off. He would have to rely on his heavy hunting boot instead.

He was hyperventilating now and felt slightly dizzy because of it. He tried slowing his breathing, shook his head vigorously. Better.

Raising his right foot high, he waited for her to come within range. He knew he would have to make it his best shot. No telling how many more opportunities there would be like this one, if any. His eyelids felt stretched and his eyes as if about to pop out of their sockets. Closer and closer she came, at breakneck speed, and yet it seemed to be taking forever. He lifted his leg higher still, until he felt the pull in his groin. Just a little nearer.

There! Now! She was where he wanted her. SLAM! His foot came down with all the force at his command. Shattering pain, like an electric shock wave, shot into his ankle, up the calf, and into his knee and upper leg. He thought the leg might collapse under him.

"Son of a bitch!"

The rat had veered at the last split-second. He had lost her, and likely his best opportunity.

In despair, he swept the room with the flashlight, but with waning hope that he could ever find her in all that mess. Then, unexpectedly, the beam picked her up, darting in and out of the labyrinth of tunnels she had either built for herself or found ready-made under those numerous piles of forgotten matter. He tracked her closely, unwilling to lose her again.

She broke into the clear, zeroing in on her target for the second time. Bart thought he saw that her mouth was open, exposing those lethal, curved yellow tusks, ready to chomp into any part of him instantly on contact. Spontaneously, he drew back his still throbbing right leg, as would a football player preparing to boot a field goal.

"Yi-a-a-a! Yi-a-a-a!" he bellowed once more and smashed his foot into her broadside. She gave under the impact like an underinflated soccer ball and felt about as heavy. She let out a prolonged, agonized gasp as if she were a rapidly deflating inner tube and flew through the air, crashing resoundingly against the north wall.

It was inconceivable that any living creature could survive such a blow. But no sooner had she landed on the hard floor than she reestablished her bearings and corkscrewed into the nearest hole she could find in the foundation wall.

Not once relinquishing his fix on the hole, Bart vaulted over the several mountains of stuff standing in the way and jammed the fireplace poker into the wall after her.

"THERE, God damn you! *Now* I've got you!" he exulted, as astounded as he was pleased at this extraordinary turn of fortune. He had accomplished the impossible. She was blocked.

But there was more to do before the victory celebrations. The remaining baby rats under the furnace had to be tended to and so did the uncapped sewer pipe.

Bart found a three-foot-long piece of floor planking to substitute for the poker and promptly went to work. As before, he stroked each victim forward individually, gave it a solid whack on the head and pushed it over the edge. He waited for the splash before going for the next. After the last, he turned to the cap.

Without the pressure on him, he ran into no resistance whatever from cap or pipe, mating them easily. He used the square bolt cast as a part of the top to secure the two tightly with his fingers. The end was in sight.

He was wondering if he should telephone Meg right

away to share the good news and, better yet, to tell her he would be coming up for the weekend after all. She would certainly be pleased. He gave the cellar a final check and started to reach for the string hanging from the ceiling fixture.

Unexpectedly, a grinding sound broke the hush, as if metal were scraping against stone, followed by a dull clunk! It came from the north foundation wall. He wheeled. The poker had dropped out—in its stead, the rat's snout, its eyes flashing, nose and whiskers twitching.

"JESUS GOD!" Bart roared, springing for her, flailing the piece of planking like a wild man. The rat slithered from the hole and dropped to the ground, scooting under the closest refuge.

Bart was astride the pile instantly, swinging madly, occasionally striking something, sending it flying. The rat broke into the open, very near the dollhouse. Bart took another ferocious swipe at her, missed, sheared off the chimney at its base. "Goddammit!" he shouted at her, blaming her for the mishap, swung and missed again. She scampered under the furnace, obviously searching for her missing babies, and out the other side.

Bart, a better-than-average ballplayer in his day, took careful aim with the flashlight and hurled it at her with all his might. Rhythmically, its beam spun round and round, like the light atop an emergency vehicle, fixing the fleeing rat once a revolution.

The action felt in suspended animation, as projectile and target closed on each other. Bart had given the rat plenty of lead to compensate for her speed. He held his breath.

CRASH! The flashlight smashed against the wall, a split-second too late.

The rat immediately altered course sharply, from flight

to attack. Bart gripped the piece of floor planking more firmly, stepping out to meet her. He had the room now to deliver the final blow.

He planted his feet fast to the ground, raised the piece of planking high, as if he were going to take a one-handed golf swing, and let fly.

There was a sickening crash and the tinkle of shattered glass spraying about the room. Plunged into total darkness, but for the triangular sliver of bluish light from the playroom, Bart thought he might literally die of fright, realizing the rat would be marshaling her forces to take advantage of the dark in which she could see so well, and he not at all.

He bounded for the door, careening, stumbling, the miscellany of stuff slipping and sliding underfoot, skinning his shins, causing him to twist his ankles. He was sure the rat would be close on his heels. It was taking an eternity to reach the fire door and possible freedom. Finally, thank God, he was there.

Bart grabbed for the knob. The door held, jerking him up short, halting all forward movement. Oh, Jesus Christ! It was tied back. He tugged and tugged. Now, he could actually hear the rat closing in on him from behind. He felt he was choking, unable to pull the oxygen he needed into his lungs. Another yank at the door, this one born of outright terror. The string snapped; the door thundered shut.

The rat thumped into it on the other side.

EIGHT

BART SLUMPED against the fire door, panting, his chest feeling it was clamped in a giant vise. A shaft of pain shot across it, radiating deep into his armpit and down the length of his left arm. The tips of his fingers tingled. But he was safe. He closed his eyes.

Suddenly, the rat started gnawing at the base of the door. Bart sprang away from it, stared in disbelieving horror at the spot. He could have sworn the grinding was so violent it made the whole door vibrate.

"Stop that! Stop that!" he shouted at her, kicking at the spot repeatedly with full force. She did, as abruptly as she had begun. Bart ran upstairs to the kitchen, slamming the stairwell door behind him, and collapsed into the Victorian love seat.

He needed a drink badly. Furthermore, he felt entitled, every bit as much as so many of his colleagues who could scarcely wait for the noon hour to rush out of the bank for their first of the day. But Bart had always prided himself in not being among them, of drinking only for the pleasure, never as a crutch. And so, he deposited his hunting clothes where he had been sitting and settled for a nice, long shower instead.

His arrival at the office was so late that everyone pretended not to notice, that is, until he was out of sight in his office and it was safe for them to exchange silent looks. Midafternoon, a subordinate stuck his head through the door to inquire about something. By the quality and content of the question, Bart knew he had been dispatched as an emissary by the others. He took pains to answer, so that the correct impression would be carried back.

But his mind was far away. He had trouble focusing on the material he tried to make himself read and even more in absorbing it. He thought of going back to Clete. No. It would look like crawling. Why give him the satisfaction? No. Bart could and would do it alone. To hell with him!

"Oh, God!" he uttered aloud before he could catch himself, quickly getting up from his desk and going to the water cooler as a cover-up.

The second time he inadvertently did the same a half hour or so later, his secretary was at the door.

"Mr. Hughes, are you all right?"

"Yes. Yes, everything's fine," he replied confidently.

"Is there anything I can do...I mean, do you need anything?"

"No, no, really, thanks. I've just got a lot on my mind, that's all. I'm sorry I disturbed you."

"I must say, you don't look so awfully well. To be honest, I've sort of felt that way about you for several days now. You sure everything is all right?"

"Yes. Please don't worry about it. Everything is just fine, believe me."

"Well, if there's anything..."

"There is nothing...thank you," he said sharply, his

patience at an end. She looked crestfallen. "I'm sorry," he said, "I didn't mean to snap at you."

"Oh, that's all right. It's only that I worry about you when you're not yourself."

"And I appreciate your concern. Really, I do. But I'll tell you, I'm damn glad it's Friday. I can surely use a couple of good nights' sleep."

Within an hour more, the office had emptied and he was alone. In no hurry to return home, he puttered about on sundry make-work projects, and then leisurely meandered up Fifth Avenue, along Central Park. It was a beautiful evening, and with the rush-hour crowds and weekend commuters already gone, New York was at its best. At Seventy-second Street he cut across town, toward the river.

Bart had long had a not-so-secret love affair with hardware stores, particularly the large, richly stocked ones. He could spend hours in them with no effort, and indeed had often thought that one day he would like to run one of his own, at retirement perhaps. All those tools of infinite variety, size, and shape, displayed in patterns of neatly descending order along the walls, appealed to the strong neat streak that ran through him. They were so businesslike, no frills, demonstrating conclusively that with the correct implement, anything was possible.

His favorite was in the middle of the block, between Seventy-second and Seventy-third Streets on Lexington Avenue.

Bart's intended purchases were not complicated, and he was therefore able to make his selections easily and quickly: a Ray-O-Vac camper's flashlight and a two-hundred-watt bulb as replacements for those he had smashed, plus workmen's gloves to substitute for the rubber ones shredded by the rat. But he nevertheless contrived to linger on well after, finally having to be shooed out by the manager telling him it was already past closing time.

During the day, Bart had concluded it was of the gravest importance psychologically that he not reveal to the rat the true depth of his fear of her. He felt that their morning encounter had essentially ended in a draw, but from here on, she must be made to sense Bart's overwhelming confidence in the inevitable outcome of this battle. This meant he must act assertively, demonstrating at all times not only that he was unafraid, but also that he had a plan of action and that he intended to see it through come what may.

And so, arriving home, he discarded his customary entry technique as too revealing and strode without pause from the street directly to the kitchen. Continuing to play to his gallery downstairs, he moved about noisily, purposefully, as the man in charge, who knew what he was doing. He prepared the traps, dressed for battle and, ready, set off immediately for his destination. Without allowing time for second thoughts, he pushed open the fire door, and waited, on the razor's edge, looking around, searching, wondering, holding his breath, too curious to be frightened.

Nothing happened. He stepped inside.

To facilitate travel, he had gathered the seven loaded but uncocked traps, the box of poison, and the replacement bulb into one brown paper grocery bag. This freed his other hand for the new flashlight and piece of three-foot planking, still his substitute for the fireplace poker.

He moved quickly to the center of the room, put the bag at his feet, took out the bulb, and reached up to unscrew what remained of the old one from the white ceramic fixture directly above him. Like a thunderbolt, a fearful buzzing sensation slammed into his fingers, shot up through the elbow and into the shoulder. He came close to letting go the new bulb, groaning as much in shock as in pain, shaking his right hand furiously, again and again.

In the terrible light, he had grossly underestimated the distance to the ceiling and had jammed his fingers into what was in effect a live electrical socket. He was having no luck!

Although badly shaken, he tried again. This time it went smoothly, and the brilliant light that inundated the room as a result somehow made it seem all worthwhile.

His starched new workmen's gloves made cocking the traps awkward, but in due course he got the hang of it and the job completed. He distributed five as originally planned along most important travel routes. The sixth went where the baby rats had been, near the furnace.

The seventh he wanted to locate at the base of the north wall, just beneath the hole into which he had seen her corkscrew. He approached it watchfully, half expecting her to burst from it momentarily. The fireplace poker lay as she had pushed it out, and just where he intended to put the trap. Quickly, he recovered the one and deposited the other.

Bart spread the poison generously in the same general places, filling in the spaces between the traps and including a small deposit at the front door of the dollhouse as he had promised himself, switched the light off and pulled the door snug. Only then did he permit himself to wonder about the rat, where she had been, why she hadn't made a move against him, not so much as a sound to reveal her presence. Never mind. He was out of there, safe, and the job he had been dreading all day was behind him.

He scooped up the day's mail which he had left on the

island counter and headed for the bar upstairs, actually no more than a converted closet with a sink and an icebox and some shelves in it. Bart fixed a double and disregarded the ritualistic "drop of water" that normally accompanied his nightly scotch on the rocks. He had waited since early morning for this one.

Clutching the glass in his left hand, preliminarily sorting the mail with the thumb and forefinger of his right, he aimed for his favorite comfortable chair in the library. Meg considered it a monstrosity, more suited to the attic, but Bart had loved this old chair as long as he could remember.

It was an oversized dark green leather affair that had belonged to his grandfather. He could still recall as a child peering into the old gentleman's study and catching sight of the shiny pate peeping over the top and the elbows jutting out at each side. It meant DO NOT DISTURB! as plainly as if the words had been spelled out in bold relief the width of the chair's backside. Undaunted, Bart would barge ahead. His grandfather would lay down the Greek classic he had been reading, lean over and clamp his huge hands around Bart's chest in preparation for the long journey up and into his lap. Then, they'd talk about life.

Bart could tell at a glance that the mail was running true to summer form, the typical assortment of bills and junk. But he knew, too, that in his engulfing solitude, he would devour each piece as if convinced it would yield some hidden treasure.

Anticipating the bliss of sinking into his beloved chair, he relaxed back and leg muscles simultaneously and let himself go. He dropped, right on through, not stopping until cushion, springs, webbing, horsehair and himself were all sitting on the floor together. The mail flew from one hand, the glass from the other, spraying scotch and ice cubes over his head and all over the leather-bound volumes in the bookcase behind.

Bart had been nursing the old chair along for years, knowing that it was in poor health and its days consequently numbered. But he had never suspected the end could be so near.

Wedged as he was within its wooden frame, he had to pull and heave his body vigorously and kick the lower half of his legs hard in an effort to disentangle himself. Twice he was almost free, twice he fell back. In the end, he had no recourse but to throw his entire weight in one direction so as to tip the chair over and be able to crawl out, onto the floor. As it went, there was a sickening, wrenching crack. Both legs on that side collapsed under him. Bart felt sick at heart.

Suddenly, there was wild scratching under the sofa, the scurrying of something trying to gain traction on the highly polished oak floor. And there was a squeaking, the same as he had heard in the cellar, only one voice, more mature, strident.

"So, this is where you've been, GODDAM you!" Bart screamed at her, springing for the sofa bed, pulling it away from the wall. But she was not there, neither behind it nor under it. At that precise moment, the logs stacked in a large, open-ended wicker basket by the fireplace shifted position. Bart vaulted across the room, grabbing for the fire tongs next to the mantlepiece. Again, the logs grunted.

As if crazed, he threw the tongs aside and clawed at the logs, hurling them every which way, not caring where they landed. It was plain madness for him to be sticking his bare fingers into where he knew her to be not inches away, but he didn't care. He was beyond caution.

In no time, the basket was empty, the logs insanely strewn about the room. Bart was panting heavily. He stood back, glowering at the basket. Then, clickety-click, click, clickety-click. Minute particles of grit were being flaked loose inside the chimney and pinging onto the logs resting in their cradle, ready for burning.

"I'll fix you, you rotten bitch!" Bart cursed at her and put a match to the crumpled paper under them.

The dry logs, long there, crackled and popped, the flames licking upward. The room began filling with smoke. Bart had forgotten about the trap, high in the flue. It was closed for summer.

"I must be losing my mind!" he chided himself, rushing to the bar for water with which to put out the fire.

Calm restored, he shoveled the soggy mass from the fireplace into a wastebasket, restored the logs to where they belonged in the wicker basket and vacuumed the mess he had made on the carpet. Lastly, reluctantly, he turned his attention to his grandfather's chair.

Much of its innards had been shredded in a manner reminiscent of the rubber gloves, and interspersed profusely throughout were those telltale droppings.

As for the cushion itself, it, too, had been disemboweled.

It was as if the rat had deliberately singled out Bart's most cherished possession and then, with diabolical cleverness the cruelest touch of all, contrived to have him be the one to cause its ultimate demise.

"Goddam you! Goddam you! Goddam you!" he cursed her, knowing that something of him had also died with his old friend.

Bart drank more than he should have, considerably more, but it did help him to fall asleep quickly and to stay that way until he felt those eyes. They were fixed on him, so black, bottomless, unblinking, without trace of emotion. He figured he must be in a dream. Perhaps. He was so terribly far away, yet he could tell he was in his bedroom, and not alone. What time was it? He smelled that distant odor, the same as had wafted from the pipe in the cellar, only not so pungent. Was that breathing that he heard, deep, rhythmic, patient, that of someone or something who knew time was on his side? Bart fought to come alive.

A light but persistent breeze had lowered the night's temperature to more pleasant levels, but also necessitated the use of a bed sheet. Bart glanced at the clock on his bedside table. It was two-thirty-six. That ghostly glow a sleeping city throws off in the night filled the bedroom window and delineated the vague outlines of the desk near it. The breeze made the leaves of trees outside ripple nervously and their shadows dance erratically on the ceiling. The drapery at the window heaved laboriously. Several pages of a book fluttered noisily before flipping over.

Bart was lying on his back, not daring to breathe, lest he draw unnecessary attention to himself. Little by little, he raised first one eyelid, then the next, and rolled his eyes far over to the right, thinking, hoping he could stretch their horizon beyond the edge of the bed and onto the floor, without having to move his head. They creaked in their sockets, wouldn't reach. Slowly, imperceptibly, he tilted his head until he could see what he wanted. There was nothing. It must have been a nightmare.

Suddenly, a dull PLOP! over by the open window, then rustling, scratching, the same kind as he had heard downstairs, on the bare oak floor behind the sofa, more rustling. It had not been a dream. He had not been hallucinating.

The rat had fallen or jumped into the metal wastebasket next to the desk and couldn't get out. Bart's mind was racing, trying to decide what to do. He wanted to go after her, but his instinct held him back. He had nothing close at hand to use as a club, nothing which could serve as a lid to imprison her in the wastebasket. He had to decide; time was running out. The rustling and scratching reached new intensity, a clear sign the rat was growing hysterical over her confinement.

Thoomp! Light rustling. Then, silence. It was too late. She had managed to tip over the wastebasket and was somewhere on the carpeted floor.

Was she looking for him, coming to repay him for the decimation of her family? Bart wanted to leap out of the bed, to escape somehow, before she had figured out where he was. But how could he dare put his bare feet on the floor without the vaguest notion of where she might be?

He opted to stay put instead, seeking what refuge he could under the bed sheet held taut against his chin, staring wide-eyed into the blackness of the room which was working so demonically in collusion with the rat. He concentrated his full energies to doing nothing which she could misinterpret as provocative.

Bart had a blinding headache. The terrible throbbing had grown so loud, he was sure she could hear it, too. Vainly, he sought to suppress it. He wondered where she had gotten to by now. There had been no sound from her since she had upset the wastebasket. Pinioned there in his bed, he was entirely at her mercy. Oh, God! There was nothing he could do but wait.

He would not have to for long.

The first in a series of sharp tugs pulled on the sheet pressing against the tips of his toes. The strong, jerking movements reminded him of how a fishing bob will jiggle with each nibble at the bait.

"Oh, Jesus God, help me!" he whimpered half audibly.

He was bathed in an icy sweat. That terrible vise he had first experienced outside the cellar clamped around his chest again. He wanted to move, but was frozen with terror, his muscles refusing to respond. He thought he might choke from fright, fought to pull air into his lungs.

The rat kept tugging at the sheet.

"Oh, God! Oh, God!" he cried out in anguish.

Why didn't she do what she had come to do and get it over with? Only to torture him, to hold him in agonizing suspense, to drag out her revenge, his punishment?

The vise tightened, a shaft of pain pounded into his armpit. The palm of his left hand tingled along with the tips of the fingers. He was sure of it now. This was the end. He was about to die.

Then it came. She thumped heavily onto the foot of his bed. Bart yelped like an injured dog.

He felt her scud between his outstretched legs. It made no difference that he could not actually see her. The smell she carried getting stronger and the depression her moving body made in the sheet told all. He knew precisely where she was.

Resolutely, she pressed her purpose, initially in silence, but then accompanied by an excited squealing, gleeful, diabolic, gloating. What Clete had said about rats preferring to attack softest body parts first flashed into his head. He moved instantaneously to shield his perilously vulnerable groin from her with his left hand.

Bart fought to keep his head. The sheer will to survive took over, forcing his muscles to respond this time. Slowly he started to pull himself stiff-leggedly out of her path, using his right hand to push with. But she kept pace absolutely, until she had him sitting bolt upright against the headboard, with nowhere further to retreat. She held him there for what felt to him a lifetime, braced for the inevitable, praying that it wouldn't hurt too much, that she'd be satisfied with inflicting only a minor wound.

"Do it, goddam you!" he begged her, shivering, whimpering, still cupping his groin protectively.

Suddenly, without warning, the pressure on the sheet released. She was airborne. Instinctively, Bart threw his arm across his eyes, simultaneously diving to the right. He had a fifty-fifty chance of it being the safest direction. She thudded into the headboard and landed on the pillow next to him. He smelled her go by and felt her heavy, furry body graze his left shoulder.

Had he held his ground, she would have hit her target dead center, square in the face.

Bart flung aside the sheet covering him and lunged for the lamp on the bedside table. In his desperation, he hit the shade. The lamp wobbled precariously. He groped for the switch, but the socket containing it kept spinning from his fingers. At any second, he expected to feel the rat by his side clamp her incisors into his naked haunch. "Oh, dear God! Please! Please, dear God, help me!" Mercifully, the bulb ignited. Bart felt his pupils rushing to contract in the contrasting brightness.

In a flash, he was standing by the bed, breathing rapidly, excited, frightened, relieved, indignant, thankful.

The headboard wavered. He sprang for it, palms extended. With a modicum of luck, he might yet be able to mash her flat between it and the wall behind. No more than an inch and a half separated them. But there was no resistance. Had it been an optical illusion in the fever of excitement? Or had she been there and managed to escape? No time to decide.

Movement under the sheet, something tunneling. Bart pounced onto the burrowing target, pummeling it frenziedly with his clenched fists. Again, she eluded him.

"Where are you, goddam your soul?" he screamed at her.

PLOP! It came from the bathroom, as if in answer, followed a moment or so later by tha-lump...tha-lump...tha-lump...

Bart catapulted for the hallway outside his bedroom, grabbing a shoe from the closet nearby in passing, leaned over the banister, glaring into the black stairwell. Tha-lump...tha-lump...tha-lump came from below, fading.

"God DAMN you!" Bart yelled, firing the heavy shoe at her from where he stood as hard as he could. He was without his armor and without weapon. It would be utter insanity for him to chase after her now. Yet, he needed some way to work off his anger, his frustration, the terrible fright she had given him.

One final tha-lump, and she was gone.

Bart stared after her, or rather into the total blackness. His knees felt wobbly, his arms leaden, his stomach uncertain and, although stark naked, he was drenched in an alternating hot and cold sweat.

He retreated to the bathroom, and without bothering to switch on the light, filled the basin with cold water. Using both hands, he scooped all he could into them and sloshed the contents into his face. More than water there. Instantly, he felt the wall for the electrical switch. The light came on.

Rat droppings were floating about in numerous clusters on the surface, a few just beginning to break free and to spiral toward the bottom. A subconscious signal impelled him to raise his head and look at himself in the mirror above. One dropping was mashed against his forehead, another stuck to his eyelid, yet another, loosening itself, fell off his upper lip.

"Oh-h-h, God!" he wailed, as his knees buckled under

him. He barely reached the toilet in time. Wrapping his arms around the bowl for support, he proceeded to heave his guts out.

When he could no more, he struggled to his feet and, propping himself against the basin, lifted the center lever. He felt as wrung out as after a prolonged illness in bed. Even so, he could not take his eyes off the rat droppings until the last had swirled around, past and through the chromium drain plug.

Now, for the first time, he noticed what further vengeance the rat had wrought. His tube of toothpaste had a jagged, gaping wound in its side. Its turquoise entrails oozed through it and serpentined down the side of the basin. The bar of soap had been lacerated almost beyond recognition and his toothbrush chewed into bits. Even the plastic water glass had not been spared, bearing repeated evidence of the rat's relentless gnawing all around its rim and flanks.

But Bart was too whipped to react. He staggered back to his room and fell onto his bed. He heard a fire engine crying in the distance, or perhaps it was an ambulance. Somebody else in trouble like him. Only they were getting help.

Whatever else the rat had proved, it was patently clear to Bart that she no longer viewed their engagement as merely a struggle for survival. For her, it had escalated into a personal vendetta.

PART TWO

NINE

"BUT YOU DON'T UNDERSTAND!" Bart protested vigorously, a touch of panic showing.

He was talking with the man who had answered the telephone at Allright Exterminators, Inc., a name he had found in the Yellow Pages.

Bart had not been able to fall asleep after the rat's attack or, more exactly, he had not dared, sitting up in his bed for the rest of the night while the lamp on his bedside table burned and the television blared for companionship. At eight o'clock he picked up the phone and started dialing one name after another. Allright had been the first to come alive.

"Where do you get off saying *that?*" the man demanded testily. "I been in this business a long time and been dealing with rats..."

"Yes. I'm sorry," Bart interrupted, backtracking as fast as he could. "I didn't mean that the way it sounded."

"Well, all right, then."

"Just listen to me, will you? Just listen."

"So, I'm listening," the man agreed unhappily.

"This rat's out to get me, I know that now."

"Aw, now, come on, mister! Why would some rat want to go and do something like that to a nice-sounding fella like you?"

"Because I knocked off her family, that's why," Bart parried, choosing to disregard the humoring.

"You did *what?*"

"I killed all her kids...every goddam lousy one of them...and she's pissed off as hell at me for doing it. Wants to pay me back. Jesus! You can understand that, can't you? I mean, how would you feel if it was your kids involved?"

"Not good, that's for sure," the man said lightly, adding after a pause, as if thinking aloud, "Still, I suppose it could happen at that."

"I'm telling you it *did* happen," Bart insisted, overhearing. "Last night."

"Oh?"

"That's right. She climbed up to the third floor...right to my bedroom...and jumped on the bed and came after me."

"Yeah?"

"I thought sure she was going for my...uh...my balls," Bart stumbled self-consciously. "But, thank God, she was more interested in my eyes."

"Thank God, like you say."

"Rats do that, you know. They like the soft parts... eyes...brain...cheeks...tongue..."

"I see."

"And so, when she came barrel-assing up between my legs, naturally, I figured..."

"Naturally...of course, you would. Anybody would. But I guess you'd have told me by now if she'd gotten either of yours, right?"

"Yes. I was very, *very* lucky," Bart said soberly. "I managed to duck at the last second and she missed. But it was close as hell and I don't know if I'll be as lucky the next time, see what I mean? That's why I'm calling you."

"Mister, if you don't mind me saying so, I think you maybe got yourself the wrong guy..."

"No, no...I picked you out of the Yellow Pages. You sounded just right to me."

"Yeah, well, don't get me wrong. I sure appreciate the compliment and all that. But that wasn't exactly what was going through my mind...uh...it was more like maybe you should be talking with one of them psychological guys instead of me, know what I mean?"

"Look! I know the whole thing must sound crazy as hell to you, but it's the God's honest truth. I know this goddam rat. She'll keep trying...until either I get her, or she gets..."

"Yeah, well, like I was saying in the beginning, we don't make calls on weekends, including Saturdays."

"Oh, please! It'll require just a minute...and I'd feel ever so much better...safer...if you...it really is a matter of life and..."

"Okay!" the man broke in. "I hear you talking. Here's what I *can* do for you."

"Oh, that's great!"

"What did you say that address was again?"

Bart gave it to him. One thing he could always rely on, he thought to himself with satisfaction, was his ability to persuade others. A born salesman, some called him.

"You don't know how much I appreciate it," he added as a finishing touch.

"No sweat. Glad to do it," the man said agreeably. "So, what I'll do is put a contract in the mail and..."

"CONTRACT? What contract?"

"Oh! Didn't I mention that? I thought I did. Anyhow, we only work on contract...you know, by the year like..."

"But I need your help now...today...not a year from now...much less all the goddam time in between!"

"That could be, mister. But there's nobody does it any different in this business."

"Okay. Then, how much does *that* cost?" Bart asked, bracing for the bad news, shaking his head.

"Not too bad. Thirty-five bucks the first visit, fifteen the ones after."

"Jesus! That works out to two hundred bucks...just for one goddam rat."

"Yeah. That sounds about right"

"But couldn't you just this once make an exception, being that this is such a real emergency?"

"Nope!"

Bart's mind raced frantically to generate another, fresh sales pitch to throw into the breach, but all he could come up with was another pathetic little "Just this once?"

"Look, mister! Figure it for yourself. If we was to go answering every call that come in, we'd be having to run our asses off all over town all the time, chasing some bitty mouse here or false alarm there. Christ! There'd be no time for the *real* work...and we'd be outta business."

Bart wanted to refute the "real work" imputation, but either the strength or the will simply wasn't there. Instead, he filled his lungs to capacity, then forcibly drove all the air from them. His eyes were scratchy and strained from lack of sleep, his stomach empty and grumbling.

"Oh-h-h-h, Jesus, and goddammit to hell, anyway!" The man was unmoved. "So, which is it gonna be? You want the contract or no?"

Even though it was plain to see that his cause was lost, Bart dearly wanted to think of something more to say, anything which might keep this last link to the outside alive and with it, the faint chance of getting someone to share the burden, relieve the awful loneliness. All he could think of was a feeble "Uh..." « sure...I guess."

"That's what I thought," the bully gloated. "Then, once you get it, you can look it over and if you like what you see, sign it in two places. Payment of sixty-five dollars for the first three months is due then, too. Soon as we get it, me or my partner'll call to set up an appointment and..."

"Holy Christ! You're talking a week or ten days at that rate," Bart objected strenuously.

"Probably."

"Oh, hell, never mind, then!" Bart said acidly.

"Suit yourself, mister...still and all..."

It sounded to Bart as though the man was having second thoughts, faced with the imminent loss of a potential client, and was looking for a way to keep the door open.

"Yes?" Bart obliged him willingly.

"Have a nice day!"

"Oh, for...!" Bart sputtered helplessly, slamming the receiver into the cradle. "Lousy bastard!"

Angrily, he reached for the Yellow Pages and went back to dialing all the numbers he had tried before and the rest he hadn't gotten to. But his results did not improve. Either he elicited the same response in substance, or none at all. Finally, he had to abandon the effort.

Bart sank into the Victorian love seat. His body ached with fatigue. Even his head felt wobbly, too heavy for the muscles supporting it. Slowly he allowed it to drop backward until it touched the wall behind, cool and refreshing. His stomach was rumbling constantly now. And small wonder. He had not eaten supper the night before, and what remained undigested of lunch he had thrown up in the wake of the rat's savage visit.

The only food in the house was what he was keeping in the refrigerator to bait the traps. He thought of getting it, but, hungry as he was, there was something obscene about eating food intended for a rat. No, he would have to go out. Later, in a few minutes, when he felt a little stronger, he thought, closing his eyes, sighing deeply.

Suddenly, fierce gnawing nearby, soft, cadent, insistent.

Had he drifted off and been dreaming? He opened first one eye, then the other, sat up and cautiously slid off the love seat, onto the floor. On his hands and knees, he began to make his way toward the sound, detouring by the island counter momentarily to scoop up the iron fireplace poker and the Ray-O-Vac flashlight which he had left there, got back on course.

The gnawing grew more fearsome as he neared the radiator. He pressed his ear to the ground, heard it clearer still, edged ahead, praying the floor would not creak, give him away. With a modicum of luck, he could deliver a fatal wallop before she had even awakened to her peril. His heart was pounding furiously, into his temples. He dropped onto his belly, crawled forward, like a soldier on patrol through the bush. The gnawing persisted unabated, but his luck held, too. Not a sound.

At a safe distance, he put his ear to the floor again, simultaneously squinting through the louvered radiator grille. The gnawing was so near, it actually vibrated in his ear, yet he saw nothing. If he used the flashlight, the element of surprise would be lost. He knew that, but what choice was there? He clicked it on. The gnawing stopped.

The light Bart held lit up the space behind the grille. He thought surely she would be there. But she wasn't. The gnawing resumed, more intensively than before. Bart searched on. She had selected her hiding place with a diabolical cleverness.

"Where are you, goddammit?" he demanded, venting his frustration aloud. She paid no attention, continued her work. Bart feared she would break through the floor at any instant. "Stop that! Stop that! Stop that!" he yelled at her, accompanying each command with a sharp rap against the radiator grille with the poker. She obeyed one time only, the first.

Hurriedly, he donned his fighting gear. Her gnawing had grown sporadic now, as if she were pausing periodically to take a reading on his progress. Or was that some form of teasing?

He hurtled down the playroom stairs, came to the barn-red fire door, suffered a bad case of cold feet. A large lump formed in his throat. He swallowed hard twice, gripped the poker and the flashlight in his left hand, the knob with his right, and slammed his hip into the door. He listened attentively for the gnawing. It had stopped.

Bart found a small chunk of wood and used it as a prop for the door. The silence in the room was stifling and ominous. Quickly, he headed for the far end, scanning the ceiling with the flashlight, down the center, along the edges. She must be up there somewhere. He extended the search to encompass tire traps and the poison. They were undisturbed. He made a mental note to freshen the bait sometime soon.

He arrived at the back wall, directly beneath the radiator upstairs. There was nothing out of the ordinary. Kneeling down to inspect the hole into which she had plunged the night before, he shone the light into it, probed with the poker. Neither action revealed anything.

Suddenly, a pinging on his pith helmet. More like grains of sand or grit raining down from above.

Cautiously, he raised his head, allowed his eyes to course up the bare stone wall. They reached the ceiling. He was gripping the poker so tightly his knuckles had turned white.

There it was.

Without taking his eyes off it, he felt for the flashlight which he had temporarily placed on the floor by his left knee, picked it up, aimed. It was the rat's tail all right, long, naked, scaly, poking through a hole where the wall abutted the ceiling. She was swishing it back and forth at him, mocking, insolent, taunting.

Gradually, discreetly, Bart stood up, being ever so mindful to avoid telegraphing his intentions. He closed one eye, took aim, and delivered a murderous swipe at the target. An electrifying shock shot into his hand as the poker and the stone wall made contact.

"Umh!" Bart groaned.

The rat let out an agonized squeal.

She had pushed her luck too far, overstayed. The tail vanished. Bart wondered if he might not have sheared it off.

In her frenzy to escape, she sprayed another load of grit and filth into his upturned face. He coughed, tried to blink the dirt from his eyes.

He could hear her sharp claws scraping abrasively, like nails on a blackboard, against the bare tin sheets which the ceiling was made of. Bart chased after the sound, jabbing the poker as though he were delivering a two-handed uppercut, hoping somehow to break through somewhere and inflict further injury.

Then, abruptly, all scratching ceased. Bart knew she had made her escape into the labyrinth which separated the ceiling from the floor above it. But it was not important.

Bart was ecstatic. He had won a round, given as good as he took, evened the score somewhat. It was a solid victory, small though it was, and it tasted just fine.

But he did not have long to relish it. Almost at once, he was assailed by the dreadful realization. The net effect of what he had done was to worsen his situation. She was hurt, and like any injured animal, this could only lead her to greater excesses, to becoming even more dangerous.

On his way upstairs he realized the excitement had taken the edge off his appetite, but had kindled his desire for a drink. Stopping at the little bar, he poured himself a double scotch, which he as promptly downed in one swallow, straight from the jigger. The liquid seared his throat and hit the pit of his stomach like a delayed-action bomb. He flushed. His eyes watered. He poured another, emptying the bottle. But this time, he took it in several swallows, moved on.

Arriving at his room, he pushed the door snug, pulled the draperies to shut out the sunlight and quite literally fell onto his bed, exhaling a loud, plaintive "God! Where will it all end?"

Already, the scotch was beginning to do its work. The fireplace poker was snug at his side, reassuring, at the ready in case of emergency. He closed his eyes, and was asleep. It was shortly past nine-fifteen in the morning.

When he awoke three hours later, his head was throbbing, he ached from the base of his neck into the sockets of his eyeballs, his mouth tasted foul, his muscles and joints both were stiff and sore. In a word, he was badly hung over and, to make matters worse, ravenous.

Bart dragged himself into the bathroom, dropped a pair of Alka-Seltzer tablets into a glass of water, watched them fizz for a moment and sent them on their mission. They tingled gaily down his throat. Then he splashed cold water into his face, contemplated shaving his day-and-a-half growth of beard. To hell with it, he decided. Not worth the bother. Without his toothbrush or toothpaste, both of which the rat had destroyed, he settled for rinsing his mouth rigorously with Listerine. He was coming back, starting to feel human once more.

He girded himself psychologically to quit the relative safety of his bedroom/bathroom compound and to run the long gauntlet down two flights of stairs and out of the house.

Prudently, he opened the door a crack, only enough to see into and part way down the hall. The coast looked clear. He listened carefully, "felt" the atmosphere for confirmation, was satisfied. Without delay, he proceeded down the stairs, the poker in his right hand, raised and ready, anxiously looking to right and left, dreading that the rat might drop or jump onto him at any second. Down one flight, onto the next, down it, out the front door under the stoop. He slammed it shut, slumped against it, relieved, breathing rapidly. "Made it!" he sighed gratefully, half audibly.

"Why Bartlett Hughes! As I live and breathe. What on earth might you be doing there?" It was Millicent Parkhurst. She was standing on the sidewalk, examining him closely with that look of a teacher who has just caught a boy student in the girl's locker room.

In fact, she was a teacher in a private girl's school down the block. She had been a classmate of Meg's at Wellesley and had migrated to New York from her native Boston afterward, accompanied by her tweeds, her accent, and her fierce puritan ethic. Not one had she tempered, much less forsaken, in the ten or so intervening years since. During the summer months, she felt a particular responsibility to look after the interests of her chums whose husbands were summering in the city without them. More than one stray had fallen from grace thanks to the long reach of her telephone.

"Oh, Jesus!" Bart muttered, startled, before he could stop himself. Bart couldn't stand her, and she was just about the last person he had expected to run into at this point.

"I didn't know Meg was back," she said sweetly. "May I just stick my nose in and say a quick hello?"

"No!" Bart responded, a mite too hastily, he thought and corrected himself. "I mean, no, she isn't

back." It angered him how guilty she made him feel, as if he were trying to hide something from her.

"Oh, I thought...since you were here and everything... well, never mind, it's really not important. Beautiful day, isn't it?"

"Yes."

"I always say if you have to spend the weekend in the city, it's certainly more pleasant when the weather's nice, wouldn't you agree?"

"Yes," Bart said with some sarcasm, "I think I could go along with that."

"Speaking of weekends, I was under the impression...I mean, didn't Meg tell me you went up every Friday?"

"Probably she did, yes."

"It must be dreadful when you can't go up there...for some reason," she probed ominously.

"This is my third, as a matter of fact."

Bart had wanted to tweak her with this information, to let her know he was onto her fishing expedition, but it came out wrong. Immediately he regretted saying it.

"Oh? Is there something the matter?" she persisted hopefully.

"Look, Millicent!" Bart said, tiring of the game. "If

you must know what I'm hiding in there, it's a rat. I'm fighting a rat."

"Oh, Bart, it's so like you. Always ready with a quip. What kind of rat?" she asked, alarm mixed with skepticism.

"A big bad one, with beady black eyes and razor-sharp teeth and claws, ready to…" Bart lunged at her with both hands, as if he himself were the rat on the attack.

"Oh!" she yelped, springing backward. "Don't *do* that!"

"See you around, Millicent baby," Bart dismissed her, departing with the strut of a triumphant bullfighter.

The minuscule restaurant he was heading for was around the corner. It didn't look like much to those who didn't know about it, but in fact it was a neighborhood melting pot and nerve center, especially for summer bachelors. The menu was limited but good, and the price unfailingly right. Everybody knew just about everything about everybody, and everyone was on a first-name basis. It was called Sals' Place, appropriately enough, inasmuch as both owners answered to that name. Bart had not been there since before the Fourth of July weekend.

Sally greeted him warmly, as he slid onto a stool at the counter. Despite its being well into the lunch hour, he was the sole customer.

"Business is slow, eh?"

"Not really," she answered. "A lot of people away, that kind of thing. How come you're around, by the way?"

"Troubles at home," he said vaguely, hoping it would suffice. He was not at all keen to go into it.

"Sure sorry to hear that, Bart…really am." He was studying the price chart overhead, or rather, feigning it, since he had already made up his mind. "What'll it be?"

she asked gently, holding her order pad and pencil at the ready.

"Make it a bowl of beef barley, the stew sounds good, and a milkshake...chocolate...two scoops of ice cream, if that's okay."

"Appetite's good, I'll say that for him." She laughed easily, relaying the order to her husband in the kitchen as she wrote.

"Hi, there, Bart!" Sal greeted him through the open serving window. "Didn't see it was you. Just get back?"

"No. I've been here right along. Dammit!"

"Oh! I thought maybe, with the clothes, and the beard and everything, maybe you just got back from a camping trip with the family...in the Adirondacks or something."

"No. No. Family's up in Maine. But, as I was just saying to Sally, here, I've got big troubles at home right now. I took them up there over the Fourth, but I haven't been since."

"That's a damn shame, Bart," Sal' said. He and Sally exchanged glances. "But they never said it'd be easy, did they?"

Bart knew that Sals' Place was a hotbed of information, but he was truly amazed that they should already know about the rat. Maybe Clete had said something, or the delicatessen owner.

"How did you find out about *that?*" he could not resist asking.

"Jesus Christ, Bart!" Sal guffawed. "Me and Sal been at it coming onto twenty-nine years, and if you don't think we got our share of scrapes in all *that* time...MAN!"

"Best thing that ever happened to you...everybody says so...even your mother," Sally protested, affecting mildly hurt feelings. "Would you believe that, Bart...even his mother says it?"

"That's pretty good." Bart chuckled. "But that's not the kind of problem..."

"Divorce, divorce, that's all you hear about these days," Sal said, pushing the bowl of beef-barley soup through the serving window.

Bart still had little interest in going into it, but he knew he could not let matters stand as they were, not short of adding unwanted fuel to the local rumor mills.

"I've got a goddam rat loose in my house," he announced with a gravity befitting the occasion. He expected to see them react with horror.

"So?" Sal asked, with an expression to match, obviously not at all clear what all the gloom was about.

"SO?" Bart demanded, both angry and disappointed.

"So, what's the big deal? Got a rat? Get a trap," Sal said, shrugging his shoulders, starting to return to the kitchen.

"Jesus, Sal! What in hell do you think I've been trying to do...for...for the past three weeks?" He was close to shouting.

"THREE WEEKS? You gotta be kidding, Bart," Sal said through the serving window. "I never heard of such a thing. Three weeks?"

"That's what I said, Sal...it's been damn near three weeks that I've been after her."

"MAN! You're doing something wrong, that's for sure. I mean, what's so complicated about setting up a couple of traps and killing a crummy old rat?"

Bart decided to up the ante.

"And what's more, this rat has got it in for me personally. I know that for sure now...and she's just waiting for me in that house somewhere, just itching to nail me first chance she gets."

"Bart, honey," Sally ventured softly. "Rats don't come

after people like that. Only when they're cornered. You just think that."

"Yeah, Bart," Sal joined her. "That's crazy talk." He started to remove the half-empty bowl of soup, stopped, instead put down a plate heaped with large chunks of meat swimming in gravy. "Eat up!" Sal invited him, flashing a wide grin.

Bart looked at the plate, wondered where his appetite had gone.

"What about poison?" Sally asked with a smile, pouring the milkshake from the mixing container into the glass in front of him.

"Of *course* I've tried poison!" Bart bellowed impatiently. "Two kinds, to be precise, and she thumbed her nose at both of them."

He dabbled with his fork in the plate of stew, tried taking a few sips of the milk-shake. Neither would go down easily.

"Do you know where the rat hangs out, Bart?" Sal asked.

"Cellar mostly...but she gets around, too. Came right up to my room and jumped on the bed, you know. Jesus! It was really awful," Bart said, grimacing and shaking his head ruefully. "I've never been so terrified in my life."

"I can believe it, Bart honey," Sally said in a soothing voice, looking worriedly at Sal. "I can believe it...but...uh, when the rat jumped up on your bed, like you say, it didn't harm you or anything like that, did it?"

"No. I ducked...got out of the way...but just in time."

"You were pretty lucky, I'd say. Wouldn't you say that, too, Sal?" she asked in the same tone as before, shooting him a sidelong glance. He nodded. "But why don't you just do like Sal here says. Keep using the traps and the poison, and I just know everything'll be all right."

"Not with her, it won't, believe me. She's smart and tough and she knows time is on her side. All she's got to do is wait till I'm asleep or not looking or hide in some corner or under something, then, when I least expect it, jump me and nail me for sure. The handwriting is on the wall."

Bart gazed wistfully through the large front window, out into the street, then said, "Have you ever had a rat loose in *your* house, Sal?"

"Not in my house exactly...but here, sometimes, especially in the beginning, before I got the place real cleaned up, but they never got to stick around any three weeks, I'll tell you that."

"You've been lucky," Bart said sadly.

"Look, Bart! It seems to me, if you don't mind me saying so, that you're making a hell of a lot out of a thing that's pretty simple. There's nothing so goddam complicated about catching a rat. So, if it was me with the problem, and one trap wasn't doing the job, I'd get myself another and if that—"

"She's not interested in the traps, Sal," Bart interrupted him wearily, "or the poison. Can't you see that? It's me she's interested in. I'm the one who killed her kids. I'm the one she wants. Me. Me. ME! To pay me back. How *can* I make you understand that?"

Why was it so inordinately difficult to get people to believe? First, that damn exterminator and now the two Sals. Was it that they were incapable of it, or that they simply didn't want to?

Whichever it was, Bart was convinced, as a result of this exchange, that it was useless and frustrating, if not actually counterproductive, to discuss the rat with others, unless they, too, had suffered a similar experience. He resolved not to do so again and rose to leave.

"Thanks, Sal and Sal. I appreciate your trying to help," he said sincerely, realizing their inability to do so was not their fault. Quickly, he pocketed his change and departed, knowing he would not be returning soon. The food on his plate and the milk shake had hardly been touched.

When he arrived home with a new bottle of scotch and a fresh supply of toilet articles, he could hear the telephone jangling inside. He forgot about the rat for the moment, fumbled for his key, ran for it, getting there in the nick of time.

It was Meg.

"Hold on a sec. Let me catch the front door," Bart said to her. What he really wanted to do was to retrieve the poker which he had left there on his way out. On his return he sank into the Victorian love seat, the telephone pressed to his ear.

"My God! It must be mental telepathy. Am I glad to hear your voice!" he exclaimed with genuine enthusiasm. For an instant, he could not quite recall when they had last talked. Less than forty-eight hours ago? Could that be all, with so much having happened to him since?

"Really?" Meg responded, sounding dubious.

"You bet! Nicest thing that's happened to me all day. I just walked in. Went out for a bite over at Sals' Place. How is everybody?"

"Fine. How are things with you?" she asked mechanically.

"I feel I'm definitely closing in," he lied, "and so we ought to be nearing the end of this goddam ordeal."

"I hope so...for both our sakes."

"How was it at the Fharquars' last night?" he inquired, pleased at his presence of mind to remember about the dinner.

"Oh, it was all right, but as you said, those things are never much fun unless we're there together."

"Yes, I know," he said, surprised at how much he resented the terrible disparity that had come into their lives.

There was a long pause as though both of them had run out of conversation.

"Uh…" Bart started, but she stopped him.

"There were a lot of your friends there…asking about you…wondering why you hadn't been up in so long."

"Nice to know they still remember me." He laughed hollowly.

"I guess what they were really wondering was whether there was something wrong …you know, between *us*, I mean."

"People are always looking for trouble. You know that. Especially that kind. Especially up there where nobody's got enough to do."

"That's not fair at all, Bart. These were your friends asking, not mine, and they work just as hard as you do. There isn't, is there?"

"What?"

"Something wrong between us…I mean, that I don't know about? They say wives are always the last to know."

"Oh, Meg, for Christ's sake! What makes you come up with that idea?"

"When I tell people…you know, why you haven't been coming up, they look at me as if I'm some kind of fool. It's as if they didn't believe it."

"Sons of bitches! Shows how much they know about it," Bart said feelingly, hating them all.

"It seems that everyone has a favorite rat story to tell. I was talking with Mr. Rangers …down at the market…and he told me he had a rat in his garage for the longest time.

And so, he kept putting poison out there and the poison kept disappearing as fast as he could put it out and he couldn't for the life of him figure what was happening to all of it."

"I know the feeling."

"Finally, one day, after the rat had disposed of enough poison to kill ten rats, Mr. Rangers happened to be in his garage and it was when he went to change the oil in his car, he said."

"That?"

"That he found out."

"You're making it a cliff-hanger, Meg, sweetheart."

"I knew you'd be interested, the minute I heard it, and I just couldn't wait to tell you. Anyway, it seems the rat was storing the poison...for a rainy day, I guess...in the car's engine compartment. Can you believe it?"

"Yes. Yes, I'll believe anything when it comes to those goddam things."

"But Mr. Rangers said he still hadn't decided whether that was what the rat was really doing...you know, storing it...or just pulling his leg. Don't you think that's funny?"

"He's lucky to be able to laugh about it," Bart said miserably.

"You know, Bart, I can stand anything except being made a fool of."

"Try dealing with a rat."

"I don't mean that, Bart."

"What *do* you mean, Meg?" The conversation was starting to get on his nerves.

"Well, other than Mr. Rangers, no one seems to understand why it should be taking so long."

"Meg," he said with a controlled calm that bordered on the hostile.

"Everybody thinks..." she persisted, oblivious.

"Meg, darling..." he interrupted her again in the same tone as before. "Meg, 'everybody' is not who's dealing with this rat. I am."

Why was she being so insensitive? It was wholly out of character. Suddenly, it came to him.

"Meg, what are you *really* calling me about?"

"Well, Milli..."

"Goddammit!" he cut her short. "I should've guessed. And what did that meddlesome bitch say to you? Christ, she burns my ass! Sneaking up behind me, just looking to make trouble."

"She wasn't sneaking up behind you. That's just your imagination. She was only trying to be friendly...and if I may say so, you had no right to snap her head off. But that's not the point."

"What *is* the point, Meg...as if I didn't know?"

"Well, I'm beginning to think there's something funny, too, Bart. *That's* the point," she said icily.

"Good old Millicent," Bart observed acidly. "Don't you know better than to listen to that fool?"

"I don't know what to believe any more," she said sadly.

"Oh, Meg, for Christ's sake!" he responded wearily.

"What do you *want* me to think, Bart? What can I think...when Milly tells me you looked just awful...as if you were just coming in from all night out on the town?"

"That ass!"

"And that you hadn't shaved...and that your eyes were all bloodshot...as if you hadn't slept in days..."

"Oh, for *God's* sake! I don't believe this!"

"And that you were even dressed funny...as if you didn't want people to know who you were...or something..."

"Meg! These are my hunt—" He stopped himself short.

"And that you acted funny, too...as though you intended to *hide* something from her..."

"Meg!" he protested. "Listen to me, will you, dammit? This is cut out of whole cloth. How can you believe such crap?"

"You mean it's not true what she said?" Meg demanded.

Bart was in a dilemma. Much as he resented being on the receiving end of Millicent's allegations, it was not as bad as having Meg know the full extent of his peril. Ever since the onset, he had purposely sought to spare her needless worry by playing down the whole ordeal as a time-consuming, frustrating bore, nothing more. He saw no real advantage to changing that policy now.

"Well? I'm waiting!"

"Well, not exactly, Meg. What she described is true, but it's the way she described it, or took it, that's all wet."

"I see. And what about reeking of Listerine? That also 'all wet,' as you put it?"

"Oh, Meg, if you only knew the half of it..." he lamented under his breath, momentarily tempted to blurt out the truth. But she didn't hear what he said, and he resisted.

"As if *that* was going to hide the liquor you smelled of...Oh, Bart!" She sounded on the brink of tears.

"Christ! This is all I need. A rat out to do me in...and now my wife thinking I'm out tying one on or running around or something. Jesus! I wish to hell that *was* what I've been doing, I'll tell you that!"

"That's what you say, Bart," Meg said glacially, not hearing the part about the rat, "and, of course, I have no way of knowing *what* you're up to down there, but you can be sure of one thing, I don't like it one bit."

"Neither do I, Meg...even though we're not talking about the same thing. Neither do I. But obviously you've made up your mind and I heard you," he said measuredly, his patience and tolerance at an end, no longer able or caring to conceal it. "For what it's worth, you happen to be wrong, and I'm terribly sorry that horse's ass has gotten you all excited like this, but..."

"Well, how *do* you explain it, Bart?"

"I'll tell you all about it when I see you Friday. We'll have all weekend to talk," he said, feeling and sounding worn out, adding as an afterthought, "after this unbelievable nightmare is over." He wished he hadn't.

But it didn't matter. She hadn't heard that either, any more than she had heard anything else he had really been saying.

And on that discordant note, they parted, neither certain the other had said good-bye.

The rat had finally managed to close the circle, to drive a wedge between him and Meg. His isolation was total. Now it was just the rat and him. One on one.

TEN

BART STAYED WHERE HE WAS, on the love seat, for some time afterward. His legs were stretched out in front of him, his head resting against the wall behind, his hands clasped across his stomach. He stared gloomily at the telephone, wishing to God it might spring to life again and that he would find Meg there. But it was not to be.

He knew the rat had been watching him all along, and still was. Not that he could see her doing so, or anything like it, of course. But he knew it as positively as if he could. She was in that room with him, behind one of the kitchen appliances, inside a cabinet, near the radiator where he had heard her digging under the thin floor, somewhere, just sitting there, coldly keeping him under surveillance.

It was enough to madden, literally, her mastery of this technique, how she could know at all times where he was in the house and what he was doing, while revealing only the sketchiest of details, if any, about herself. She had won the initiative, the upper hand psychologically, and, with it the ultimate, tactical superiority. And he had been reduced to being constantly on the defensive, having to do battle with an elusive phantom. Bart despised her for it, but the brilliance with which she had pursued her objectives since her arrival had earned her his grudging respect as well.

He didn't think she would attack him then and there, despite her proximity. The conditions weren't right. Too much open space. Too much daylight. And so, he felt safe in closing his eyes and taking a breather.

His conversation with Meg had left him feeling morose and abandoned. But mostly, he was profoundly angry. Angry at himself for having been so slow to recognize the rat for what she was and, therefore, contributing so much to the situation mushrooming out of control. Angry at all those whose help he had sought and who had given him nothing but lip service in response. Angry at Meg for berating him at the very moment when he needed her most. And angry at that cursed rat who was at the root of it all.

He felt that his world was caving in on him and that he might easily be crushed by it. Why had the Almighty singled him out for such a terrible punishment and then joined the others in forsaking him? Bart had not cried since the day his father was buried, but now his eyes started to water and that telltale knot was building in his throat. He didn't want to and fought to overcome it.

But he was no more successful in that than he was in curtailing his unruly imagination. For the first time, that nagging question, which he had always managed before to relegate to the background, would not go away. What if the traps failed to do the job? And the poison, too? What then?

Initially, he had been able to respond with a goodly number of seemingly plausible countermeasures he could take, and his optimism would surge with each. But, one after another, they would wither under scrutiny. His spirits quickly resumed their downward spiral, reaching an apathy bordering on torpor, and beyond. At their lowest, he had actually considered that if she would just leave him alone, he would willingly reciprocate, and life under the same roof could be made bearable once more.

But this specious thinking fared no better than the rest, for in his gut, Bart never doubted what the true alternatives would be. One way or the other, one of them would have to leave.

The half-gallon bottle of scotch he had bought on the way home from Sals' Place stood on the island counter, tall and beckoning. He eyed it longingly now. He was drinking far too much these days and would have been the first to admit it, if pressed. But these were extraordinary times requiring extraordinary measures. Furthermore, scotch was well known for its medicinal properties. He succumbed to temptation and was immediately glad he had.

It wasn't as though he did not know what he should be doing instead. The bait on the traps was a day old, not a serious problem in itself, but it could benefit from a freshening. Yet, he couldn't. He could not bring himself to face that hateful cellar and the possibility that the rat might drop onto his head at any instant while he worked there. To boot, his hands were unsteady. Not a good thing when having to trigger a rat trap.

And so, he chose to retreat to his bedroom/bathroom compound, taking with him the newspaper, some work from the office, the fireplace poker and, of course, the bottle of scotch. He wanted time. Time to formulate a strategy. Time to rest and garner strength. This would be the safest place, he figured, provided there were no breaches in its defenses through which the rat might gain access.

Immediately on arrival, he undertook to assure that

this would be the case. When he was done, twenty or so minutes later, he was satisfied. The rat was not in the area. Both doors leading into it from the hallway were shut and locked. And the two potential trouble spots he had uncovered were taken care of.

The first, at the fireplace, he resolved by shoving the loaded bookcase snugly against the mantle opening. The second was slightly more problematical, since it involved a large hole surrounding the radiator pipe and he lacked anything of a permanent nature with which to block it. He settled on stacking a few heavy books over it. While this solution might not prevent her from entering, it would entail her having to push them aside and this, in turn, would alert Bart to his impending danger.

But despite these elaborate security measures, Bart could not get himself to relax. He tried listening to his favorite FM radio station, watching television, reading the newspaper or the book he had made no progress with since the day of her arrival. His attention span was zero. She kept intruding his every thought.

At regular intervals he poured himself another drink, whenever the glass was empty. This helped, at least in the beginning. It made him drowsy and encouraged him to seek the sleep he so badly needed. But no sooner would he doze off than the dreams would start.

While the rat herself was never the feature attraction of these staccato nightmares, his frustration and fear of her were unmistakably their inspiration.

In one, he tumbled helplessly down a long flight of stairs, unable to grab hold of the handrail in time to break his fall or to call out for help. In another, he raced for the last train, only to have everyone and everything stand in his way to thwart him. In yet another, by far the most chilling, he desperately sought to dissuade those who had been dispatched to do it from marching him to the wall and executing him.

Again and again, they recurred. Again and again, they awoke him with a start, out of breath, in terrified sweat, robbed of the smallest beneficial rest.

His only recourse was to reach for the bottle, but he soon realized that the scotch was not working nearly so effectively as it had in the beginning, requiring him to drink more and more just to stay at the same level of numbness.

At two-forty Sunday morning or close to it the rat had started in, scampering insanely about in the ceiling of his bedroom. At first, he thought it could have been one more of those miserable dreams tormenting him, but any such notion was quickly dispelled.

He sat bolt upright in his bed. There was no need to turn on the lights, since he had left them all ablaze since nightfall. Bart looked up at the ceiling, worriedly following her movements with his eyes. She was behaving most erratically, darting here, there, everywhere, in short spurts, interrupted by brief bursts of gnawing wherever she paused. He wondered if perhaps she had gotten into Clete's poison and was frenziedly hunting for water, crazed from thirst. But in a dusty, arid joist space? Not very likely. It had to be something else.

Then he saw it, clear as light, in one dreadful flash. She was intent on breaking into his fortress, to get at him, and was searching for the easiest spot to dig through. All of a sudden, she stopped altogether, directly above him, and settled down to gnawing in earnest. Bart knew she had found it.

He gripped the fireplace poker at his side and swung his legs over the edge of the bed, avoiding any sudden movements. The gnawing stopped instantaneously, yet he was not aware of having made the merest sound. He waited. Shortly, it resumed. To test her, he made a slight movement toward standing up. Again, she quit. How was it possible for her to know so infallibly his every move without actually being able to see him? Abruptly, hoping to catch her off guard, he sprang to his feet. Instantly, she halted.

He waited there, by the side of the bed, motionless, in absolute silence, holding the poker in his right hand, at the ready to whack the ceiling right under her the moment the grinding renewed. This would not hurt her, he knew, but it couldn't help giving her a good jolt and, hopefully, it might persuade her to desist once for all.

But the chomping did not resume as he expected. She left him standing there. One minute, another. Then three, five. Could she have given up? Bart's calves had begun to tingle and tremble from nervous stress and fatigue, and his back was aching, too. What *was* she doing up there? He dropped onto the bed, unable to stand longer on his watery legs. Silence from above. She must have gone.

Reassured, he let himself fall against the pillow, swung his legs onto the bed, relaxed his grip on the poker. The relief that coursed through his entire wretched body was unconditionally exquisite. He closed his eyes, sighing gratefully, and felt himself start to drift away.

Immediately, the rat picked up where she had left off, startling him back to life, only this time she had changed her location to somewhere over the desk at the other end of the room.

Over and over, she played this satanic trick on him, of gnawing until she had forced him onto his feet, leaving him stranded there, tense and expectant, until he would lose heart, then repeating the whole process at some new location as soon as he had regained his bed. Was she trying to drive him mad?

By the time she had finished with him, he was beyond caring what her intentions were. The electric clock on his bedside table said five-twenty-six. She had been persecuting him for close to three hours.

He lapsed into a sleep of the dead, too exhausted even to dream. That, at least, was something to be thankful for. Midmorning, he awoke listening for her, apprehensively looking up at the ceiling, more or less convinced she would be in its joist space, back at work. But she wasn't. Another thing was also apparent to him. He could not let the traps go a third night.

Bart had remained barricaded in his fortress since early afternoon the previous day. He had been a virtual prisoner there, but he didn't mind. He preferred that to having to run that terrifying gauntlet through the house, past those blackened rooms, filled with nooks and crannies where she could be lurking, claws and molars bared, poised to scurry out in front of him, block his passage and thereby goad him into unwanted hand-to-hand combat.

But now, with nothing to eat in the house, he would have to risk going out. Besides, chances were this would be as propitious a time as any. After keeping him up most of the night, she would in all probability be sleeping, garnering her strength for what further harassment she had in mind for him.

He made the sortie without incident, returning from the delicatessen with just enough food for the day (all of which he could eat in his room and thereby avoid using the kitchen) *The New York Times* (Sunday edition), a five-pound bag of granulated sugar, the biggest box of rat poison he could find on the shelf, and half a pound of raw hamburger. This last item was for her, too.

At two o'clock or thereabout, he decided he had read all he wanted of the newspaper and that he had delayed the inevitable long enough. He began his preparations for the journey into the cellar, fortifying himself, as he donned his battle dress, with three or four hefty gulps of scotch, taken direct from the bottle. They were his first of the day and impacted on him harder than he had expected. So much the better.

Swiftly, he descended into the combat zone, pausing briefly inside the red fire door for prudence sake and then briskly moved on. After detonating the seven traps with the poker, he gathered them into the brown paper grocery bag he had brought them in, and returned to the kitchen.

Bart was pleasantly surprised by how smoothly the cleaning and reloading went. Then, using a quart-sized plastic ice cream container, he stirred the poison into the granulated sugar in about a two-to-three ratio. Finally, he thoroughly kneaded a similarly potent allocation into the raw hamburger. Each of these he carefully stacked in the same paper bag for transportation downstairs.

It was tougher entering the cellar the second time; he didn't know quite why, made an extra-critical check from the doorway. All appeared tranquil. His imagination had been the culprit, he concluded, stepping out smartly.

The rat dropped onto his pith helmet with a resounding, nerve-shattering thud. The two spun in tandem to the floor.

Her cold, scaly tail grazed his bare cheek as she passed. It felt like sandpaper.

"Oh, Jesus Christ, no!" Bart begged aloud, staggering backward, the shock causing him to release the bag. It burst apart as it hit the floor, spilling its contents in a wide arc in front of him. The rat was there also.

Immediately, she set about intertwining herself in his

feet, running in ever-tightening circles, alternating with figure-eight patterns, first in one direction, then switching without warning to the other. Clearly, she wanted to make him fall, to bring him down to where he would be easier for her to work on, to best him for good.

Desperately, he sought to stave her off, to disentangle himself from her, jabbing with the poker at her as if he were spearfishing, hopping, dancing, lurching away, wherever there looked to be an opening. But she was too fast, too nimble, seemingly able to anticipate what he would do, relentlessly keeping after him. He teetered precariously off balance, narrowly saved himself by catching hold of the doorframe. She squealed merrily, racing, turning, maneuvering this way, that.

Skillfully, she piloted him along the wall, into the corner. He managed to jump clear, but she was after him at once, determined that he should not regain the open fire door and possible escape. His head was twirling, he had difficulty pulling the air he needed into his lungs, his chest felt cramped and his arm was hurting, as both had before. His fingertips had turned cold and tingling.

It could be no more than a matter of moments, and she would have him where she wanted him. He thought he might black out, made himself blink, shook his head, striving to prevent it.

The will to survive took command, as it had the night of her vicious attack in his bedroom.

He feinted to his right. She fell for it. Simultaneously, he literally flung his body backward, to his left, out the door, into the playroom, trying furiously to keep from falling, but he tripped over his cumbersome hunting boots, landed squarely on his coccyx and both elbows, knocking the breath out of him. He thought he might throw up. His head snapped back, cracking sickeningly against the hard, asbestos tile floor. He saw stars.

Despite this, his mind did not lose its clarity. She could be but a few yards behind, having recovered from his deception, racing for him, readying to pounce on his prostrate, defenseless form as soon as she was within striking distance.

He rolled, struggled to his hands and knees, scrambled for the stairwell. It was requiring every ounce of strength and energy he had in him. Finally, he was at the foot of the stairs. They had never seemed so steep, so high, so awesome to him. He started hauling, pushing, pulling, clawing his way up. In his anxiousness, his feet kept spinning out from under him. Although he had been moving as fast as humanly possible, it felt as if at a snail's pace. Oh, Jesus God! Would he never reach the top?

His eyes were bulging, feeling as though they would pop out of their sockets momentarily, and he was so tired. My God, but he was tired! If only he could stop, just for a minute, to catch his breath. Maybe there was time. But how far behind could she be? He didn't dare look back to find out. No. Better not to chance it. Two more steps.

Forcing himself to put forth one, final, herculean effort, he sprang for the top landing and through the opening. Rolling clear of the door he kicked it shut with his left leg and crumbled on the floor, gasping for air. Within seconds, he heard the rat gnawing at the base of it, on the other side.

He kicked at the spot but she was not deterred. The sound of her uncompromising munching reverberated through the hollow door. Again, he lashed out at it with what force he had remaining. Feeble though the blow was, it sufficed to make her stop.

Bart stayed poised for her to renew her assault,

prepared to greet it by another sharp smack with his foot. But instead, there was the familiar tha-lump...tha-lump... tha-lump down the wooden steps. The crisis was past, for now.

He waited until he had recovered somewhat, at least to the extent of catching his breath, and then slid back toward the island counter. Once there, he sat up, propped himself against it, tucked his legs into his chest and, utterly played out, buried his face in his arms. He could have used a drink, but the bottle was too far away, upstairs, in his bedroom.

Bart had no idea how long he had been in that position when the telephone rang, nor whether he had been fully asleep, or only at some other halfway house of the mind. It was the start of the fifth ring by the time he lifted the receiver.

"Oh, it's you, Meg," he said affectionately, though hoarsely. The welcome sound of her voice made him more than willing to forgive and forget.

"I was afraid you might be out."

In light of their conversation yesterday, the words had an ominous ring. He braced for another assault, wondering what had triggered it this time.

"No, no," he reassured her hurriedly, trying to mute it. "I was down in the cellar and I guess I didn't hear the phone right away."

"Oh," she said absently, her mind obviously elsewhere. "Bart, darling...uh...what I'm calling about is...well...Look! I don't blame you for being angry with me..."

"I'm not angry with you, Meg. I know how hard this time's been on you. As a matter of fact, I was going to call you tonight. I'm the one who's at fault."

"No, you're not. It's me. I had no right just taking Millicent's word like that."

"It doesn't matter. This thing has put both of us under a terrible strain."

"It's just that it's been so long since we've seen each other...and then, to have those people at the Fharquars' and right after that her call...I mean, it all piled in on me, you know?"

"Of course, I understand, and I appreciate your calling about it. But, it's almost over, Meg."

"Well, I think I should come down. I could leave the children with..."

"Meg! That's out of the question..."

"Bart! I really want to..."

"Absolutely not! There's poison all over the place and traps...besides, it's much too dangerous."

"Who cares about the danger? As long as I'm with you, I couldn't care less."

"But I *do* care and I'll be damned if I'm going to let you be exposed unnecessarily to it."

"I'll be careful."

"No, Meg. The answer is no."

"All right, then, I've got another idea. Why don't you leave it to the exterminator and *you* come up here until it's over?"

"I can't do that, Meg."

"Why not?"

"For one thing, the exterminator's not worth a damn. And for another, this is the rat's war and mine, and no one else's."

"That doesn't make any sense to me at all."

"Maybe not to you...but it does to me. Anyway, I wouldn't expect you to understand it, Meg."

"I mean, talking about this being a 'war' and all that."

"But that's precisely what it is, Meg."

"And what do you think exterminators are for?"

"Oh, Christ, Meg, I just don't want to talk about if any more. I'm tired, my nerves are frazzled...and so, if we can't think of something else to talk about..."

"Nothing makes any sense to me anymore."

"It's not all that complicated, Meg," Bart said, his impatience coming through. "I'm doing what I have to do and I plan to keep doing it until I get it done. It's as simple as that."

"It's just crazy. The world's gone mad...and my husband right along with it," Meg thought aloud.

Despite their best intentions, the call had gone hopelessly awry and, rather than narrowing the rift between them, it had widened it.

"Women! What the hell do *they* know?" Bart complained bitterly, after Meg had hung up. "What does *anybody* know?"

Dejectedly, he made his way upstairs to his bedroom, locked himself in and dropped onto the bed, the fireplace poker at one side, the bottle of scotch at the other, and waited.

ELEVEN

"MR. HUGHES? OH, THANK GOD!" she said, sounding on the verge of hysterics. "It *is* you! You had me worried half to death." It was his secretary.

"Wh...what time is it?"

"It's..."

"Oh, Christ!" Bart cursed, glimpsing the clock on his bedside table. It was ten past eleven Monday morning.

"We've been trying to reach you for...for over an hour and there's been no answer. Oh, thank God, you're all right."

"Of *course*, I'm all right! Why wouldn't I be?" he demanded defensively.

He caught sight of the half-gallon bottle of scotch on the floor, next to his bed. Its cap was missing and it was more than three-quarters empty. "Oh, my God!" he gasped. His head felt as though a watermelon had been compressed into it.

"Did you forget about your meeting this morning?" she inquired tactfully.

"What meeting?" Bart struggled to come all the way back.

"The one with Mr. Riverton and..."

"Oh, Jesus!" he remembered.

"Mr. Cunningham. You and he were supposed to meet in Mr. Cunningham's office at ten. I think it was to go over some personnel matters. Remember?"

"Of *course*, I remember! Something...uh...came up...I had to go out...uh...couldn't find a phone...uh..."

Sargent Cunningham was the executive vice president in charge of the entire division, of which Eliot Riverton's department formed only a part.

"It's all right, Mr. Hughes. I took care of it."

"How did you manage that?"

"I told Mr. Riverton when he came by to pick you up that you had missed your plane."

"That was quick. And what did he say?" he asked anxiously.

"He didn't seem to mind at all. Said something about those things happening sometimes...something like that."

"You're terrific! I owe you one."

"Will you be coming in, then?"

"On my way now...and...thanks."

It had been another interminable, terrible night for him. The consuming worry over what the rat would do had kept him on tenterhooks, and drinking, through most of it. Every strange creak, every unfamiliar sound of any kind, he would invariably attribute to her, bracing himself, eyes popping, and searching.

When she actually, finally, made her move in the early-morning hours, this time somewhere in the bathroom, he had greeted it almost with a sense of relief.

Since he felt he understood her game plan, he had sought to rise above it, but she would have none of that. Mercilessly, she had hounded him, ceaselessly grinding, until she had him on his feet, listening for her behind the tub, the medicine cabinet, or in whatever other concealed place he had last heard her. But, predictably, he would arrive on the scene just too late, leaving him sputtering and cursing helplessly, and inevitably driving him back to the bottle.

As with the previous night, it was approaching six o'clock before she had released him from his torment, and he had been able to find his first meaningful sleep.

Bart downed a pair of Alka-Seltzer tablets, dressed as fast as he could and hurried to the subway. He arrived at the bank around lunchtime and went directly to Riverton's office to apologize.

"Hi, El!" he said to him sheepishly, poking his head through the door.

"Good! You're here. You free for lunch, by any chance?" Eliot greeted him affably.

"Sure. You bet." He was relieved.

"Excellent! Then, let's grab a bite upstairs. That all right with you?"

By "upstairs" was meant the corporate dining room on the top floor of the building. Principally intended as an attractive place for "senior management" to entertain its clients for lunch, it commanded a spectacular view of the city, the food was the best within a twenty-block radius and, better still, it was free. Only vicepresidents and higher were entitled to use it and, with or without a customer in tow, they did so with regularity. There was no place like it for an alert, ambitious young bank officer to hobnob with the great and the near great of the corporate hierarchy. Some, not entirely facetiously, claimed it was the best thing that came with election to a vicepresidency.

"That'd be swell, El....uh...look...uh...I'm really sor..."

"Yes. Yes. We'll discuss all that upstairs. Okay?"

They rode the elevator in silence, except for Riverton's hearty greetings to the galaxy of corporate power that boarded floor by floor, destined for the same place. The maître d' bowed and led them to a table for two by the window.

"Thanks, Paul," Riverton said to him.

"A pleasure, Mr. Riverton. The bluepoints are excellent today, by the way," he said, departing immediately to tend to the queue that had been building at the door.

"See anything you like?" Riverton asked Bart.

"I'll follow your lead, El."

"I usually have the bluepoints...especially when Paul says they're good...then, the specialty of the day...oops!... not keen on spinach souffle...I think I'll have the minute steak instead...iced coffee...no dessert...but you choose what you like."

He had been writing all this down on the order slip which he had signed at the top along with the information that he was entertaining Bartlett Hughes that day.

"Sounds great to me, El. Make it two down the line," Bart said, although it was all he could do to choke down an oyster.

"Good! Two it is, then," Riverton said, putting a little "2" at each appropriate place. "Sorry you couldn't be there this morning. Good meeting with Cunningham. Too bad you had to miss it."

"Yes, I know. I'm awfully sorry about that. The goddam plane...you know."

"Yes. I heard. Funny, though, the wife and I flew down from Boston ourselves yesterday. We had no trouble with the weather at all."

Bart's blood chilled.

"We must've gotten out just in time, eh?" Eliot asked with a little smile. "Never know about the weather along the Atlantic coast this time of year. Seems to change from one minute to the next."

"I know," Bart said, nervously shifting his gaze from Eliot's, out the window. His head was throbbing as badly as when he got up, despite the Alka-Seltzer. "You look like hell, Bart, you know that?"

"I'm not surprised, El. I don't feel all that sharp either," Bart admitted. "Mind if I pass on the oysters?"

"No problem. If I didn't know you so well, I'd say you'd been hitting the sauce a little too hard. You haven't, have you?"

"No. No. Nothing like that," Bart assured him, again unable to look him in the eye. The glare through the enormous picture windows was bothering him terribly, causing him to squint. "Tired, is all. Been working too hard, I guess," he explained with a self-deprecating smile.

All along, he had been debating what he should or should not tell Eliot about the rat. He had not yet decided. The whole sorry business and his appalling mismanagement of it could only reflect badly on him.

Besides, why should Eliot be expected to understand? No one else seemed to. Better not to open that can of worms.

"Maybe you've got a vitamin deficiency," Eliot suggested firmly, as if to confirm the wisdom of Bart's decision. "Ever think of that?"

"Not really."

"Maybe you should. Happened to me once, couple of years back. Had me dragging my ass all over the place all the time. Damn near blew a promotion because of it. Then, I got straightened out."

"That was a break."

"Yes. Vitamin C. That's what did it. Anyway, let me come right to the point...why I was hoping we could have lunch together today. Maybe you know this...been able to sense it by the way I've been trying to bring you along, bring you into things...like meeting with Cunningham this morning and there could be lots more like it, if..." he paused, looking penetratingly at Bart, "if you play your cards right. I've got big plans for you, Bart, but those plans don't include messing up on me like you did today...in front of Cunningham or anyone else. When push comes to shove, it's not going to make any difference what I say. Actions are going to speak a lot louder than words. You get what I'm saying to you?"

"Yes, El. I understand."

It was common knowledge in the department that Riverton was looking for a deputy, but this was Bart's first tangible evidence that he was not only a contender, but also could be a finalist. Appointment would of course carry an automatic vice presidency, and with it, admission to the club at last.

"Now, this morning's not all that serious. Anybody's entitled to make a mistake once in a while, but I need someone I can depend on absolutely, who can act for me when I'm not around, so I know, even then, that somebody's here, minding the store. A guy who misses important obligations for whatever reason...plane connections or any other goddam thing...is no damn good to me at all."

"Yes, of course. I understand that perfectly. I'd feel the same way."

"Okay. With you, there's no need of me kicking a dead horse. Now, I'll tell you what I would like you to do. I want you to check in with Forbes Bissett...have him take a look at you...see why you're looking like hell...get to the bottom of this thing."

Bart flushed.

E. (for Elisha) Forbes Bissett III was the company doctor. Generally speaking, he was not highly regarded by the corporate multitude. Most took for granted that had he been any good, he would have been in private practice and not full time on some bank's payroll, treating chronic hypochondriacs and other hapless creatures seeking refuge from the buffetings of competitive turbulence.

As well, there was the widely held suspicion that he was more the company spy than the company medicine man. Many were convinced that he used his privileged position to extract from employees information which they would never willingly divulge if healthy and able to stand firm. The medical unit which he ran was credited with more than a few promising careers foundering in its treacherous waters.

One story about him which had withstood the ravages of time had some poor wretch going to him complaining of a debilitating head cold and severe attendant depression, only to find himself being whisked off to Bellevue Hospital for psychiatric observation. Unauthenticated, to be sure, but such was the reputation of the good doctor.

"There's no need to be bothering him, El," Bart said, stalling for time. "I'll be all right."

"Deciding on the right guy is hard enough, Bart, without the added risk of picking someone who won't hold up under pressure. That's putting it right on the line for you. It's something I want you to do. Okay?"

"Yes. Okay. Sure, El," Bart agreed quietly. He could recognize an order when he heard one.

"Attaboy! Also, I need you in top form for tomorrow."

"Tomorrow?"

"That's right. Tomorrow. I've been working on this one for months. Amalgamated Shippers and Haulers. Two hundred and ninety million. Been doing it themselves, but I guess their results haven't been so hot. Either that or they're getting antsy about Congress getting antsy…you know, about unions running their own pension funds."

"That's a nice piece of change."

"That's for sure. And I want them to have a look at the hands-on guy I think is just right to handle it," he announced his decision with a congratulatory smile. "You are free in the AM?"

"I *sure* am…and thanks for the vote of confidence, El."

"Good! Nine-thirty. And I think I'll use the big conference room. Shall we go?"

"Thanks for lunch, El." The food had in fact made him feel much improved.

"A pleasure! Give me a couple of minutes after we get back and I'll call Forbes. He owes me a favor, so I'm sure he'll see you right away if I ask him. If you don't hear from me, you just go right on up. You know Forbes, don't you?"

"No. Never met him…thank God, I suppose. Never had the occasion."

"Good guy. You'll like him."

Bart wasn't so sure.

Waiting for Riverton's call, he took care of a few odds and ends on his desk, leaving his telephone line open, hoping against hope that Dr. Bissett would be too busy, gone on vacation, anything which would make it impossible for Bart to see him. But Riverton's call did not come. It was Bart's signal to get on with it.

"I've been expecting you, Bart," Dr. Bissett said pleasantly, thrusting out his hand. "Eliot called me a few minutes ago and said you might be dropping by. Shall we sit in here and chat for a few minutes?" he asked, leading

Bart into the examining room adjacent to the reception area.

Dr. Bissett was in his early to mid-fifties, of average height, on the heavy side, with a round, cherubic face and a markedly receding hairline. Bart thought he could detect an aggressive, not to say mean, glint in the steel-gray eyes that peered through antiseptic flesh-colored eyeglasses. His smile flashed on and off like a blinker light. Bart considered it highly suspect.

"Here! Sit yourself down," Dr. Bissett said, pointing to a small white metal stool. Next to it was a table on wheels. Its top was of polished steel and on it sat a blood pressure gauge, open and ready.

Bart still felt unsteady from his heavy drinking and worried that Dr. Bissett would notice his shaking. On the long trip to the thirty-second floor, where the Medical Department was situated, Bart had reached an easy decision. He would tell Dr. Bissett nothing more than absolutely necessary and, most especially, nothing whatever about the rat.

"Now, then, Bart. What seems to be troubling you?"

"It's not trouble, really. Just a little problem getting to sleep at night, and staying that way, once I have." There was no risk involved in confessing this much of the truth.

"Oh? A young fellow like you shouldn't be having *that* kind of difficulty. Now, take an old geezer like me, well, that's something else," he said, flashing Bart a smile. "Maybe there's something eating at you, getting in the way. Anything like that that you'd care to tell me about?"

"Oh, I guess I have the same pressures as anyone else," Bart said, trying to sound casual. He was feeling better now that the game had actually gotten under way.

"Such as?"

"Promotion. Money. How I'm doing, you know, career-wise. That kind of thing."

"Yes, of course. That's natural enough and to be expected of any young man like yourself...on the rise, with a bright future ahead of him. It's people like you who provide the lifeblood to an organization such as this one. Are you always so jumpy, by the way?"

"Jumpy?" Bart jumped.

"Yes. Seems to me...well, never mind about that now. Here, let's hook you up to this contraption and see what's going on with that ticker of yours."

Bart rolled up his sleeve, and Dr. Bissett looped the gray cloth around his arm, pumping air into it. Gradually, he released the valve. Air hissed out, the pounding in his arm subsided.

"A little elevated...nothing to be alarmed over...normal, essentially, I'm happy to report," Dr. Bissett said, flashing his smile automatically.

"So am I...I mean, to hear it," Bart said, thinking he ought to acknowledge the finding in some way.

"You mean you've been worried about it?" Dr. Bissett pounced.

"No, no. Nothing like that. It's just that you never know...and it's always a relief...you know," Bart floundered, recalling midsentence the pain he had felt in his chest and arm, the tingle in his fingers.

"Yes, of course. Now, if you would, Bart, let's talk a little more about that not-sleeping business. Once you get to sleep...and I understand that this can sometimes take you a little while...but once you do, what then?"

"Then, the nightmares start."

"Nightmares? That's interesting. What kind of nightmares?"

"Bad dreams...you know...that kind of thing," Bart

answered, sensing a trap, wishing he had been able to dodge the question.

"Yes, I understand. But, could you perhaps try to be a little more specific?"

"Frustration dreams, I call them," Bart elaborated as little as he could, his mind racing to find a way of cutting the discussion short.

Dr. Bissett had not taken his eyes off him once since he had come in, except for the few seconds required to read the blood-pressure gauge. Bart felt those cold gray eyes could penetrate into his soul. He yearned to be out of there.

"That's an excellent name for them. I hadn't heard that one before. Could you give me an example?"

"Oh, you know...uh...well, for example, when you see yourself running for a train and it's the last one and everybody gets in your way or you can't find your bags or something like that. Ever had one of those?"

"Sometimes."

"And you wake up in a sweat?"

"Yes, I suppose we all have dreams like that from time to time."

"They can take other forms, too." Bart warmed to the subject, responding to Dr. Bissett's apparent interest, welcoming a chance to sound cooperative without giving away anything of substance.

"Go on," Dr. Bissett encouraged him.

"Yes. For...well, another example is the kind in which you're falling downstairs and you keep grabbing for the banister to break your fall and you keep missing and you try calling for help, but nothing comes out, you know?"

"Yes, of course. Please go on."

"That's it, really, except..." Bart had a sudden,

irrepressible impulse to tweak the lion's tail. "Yes?" Dr. Bissett went for it.

"Well, there's another in which a rat gets into my house and he chases me all over the place and no matter what I do to try to catch him, nothing works." He was careful not to use the word "she."

"That must be quite an ugly experience...frustrating, as you said."

"Yes, it is," Bart agreed, smiling inwardly at his private little joke.

"And so, what eventually happens...I mean, to the rat... and, you, of course?"

"I don't know," Bart said, caught short, no longer laughing. "I wake up in that sweat I was telling you about...you know...before the dream has a chance to end..." He retreated as fast as he could.

"Yes, I understand."

Dr. Bissett released Bart from his visual hold at last, rose and went to the large picture window. From where he was sitting, Bart could tell that the view from there was almost the same as that from the dining room where he and Riverton had lunched. That seemed so long ago. Dr. Bissett had taken out his pipe, packed fresh tobacco into it, and was holding a lighted match to it.

"You know, Bart," he turned, puffing rapidly on the pipe, sending great gray clouds into the room, "sometimes, the pressure of new responsibilities, the rising expectations of others..."

"No, no. It's nothing like that," Bart interrupted him earnestly, quickly recognizing waters even more hazardous than openly talking about the rat.

"No, of *course* not," Dr. Bissett said soothingly. "I'm only suggesting that for some of us, these pressures become too much...more than we can cope with...and this, in turn, can sometimes lead us into devising any number of ways to compensate."

"Yes, I've seen that happen," Bart said, trying to position himself on the same side, sensing that they weren't.

"Yes, I'm sure you have," Dr. Bissett continued in that same tranquilizing tone. "For example, some previously reliable employees will suddenly become chronic absentees or be habitually late getting to work. Others will turn to drugs of one sort or another. And then, there are those who start to rely too heavily on drink."

"Luckily, I've never felt the need for any of those crutches," Bart interjected urgently, inexplicably sensing the doctor was talking about him.

"No, of course not. These are hypothetical cases I've been citing, you understand. Something to keep in mind."

"Yes, I understand."

Dr. Bissett reached for a bottle the size of a gallon jug. It was filled almost to capacity with small, oblong yellow pills. He used a ladle to scoop one out, which he dropped into a dixie cup and handed it to Bart.

"Here! Take this!"

"What is it?"

"Just a little pill, Bart. There's no need of being so suspicious." He flashed his automatic smile. "It'll make you feel a lot better...take off that raw edge."

Bart went to the basin, poured water from the tap into another cup and downed the pill.

"Was that a tranquilizer?"

"Yes. You might say that. And I want you to take one every four hours for the next several days...that is, until we see each other again. Is that clear?"

Dr. Bissett ladled a number of the pills into a plastic vial, snapping the cap into the closed position.

"Here you go. Now, I must caution you, absolutely no alcohol whatsoever while you're taking these pills. And no driving. But the most important is the alcohol. Got that?"

Bart didn't like the heavy emphasis he placed on the word "alcohol," striking him again as personally directed, but he suppressed it. "Yes, surely. No problem."

"Good! Now, let's see, here." He was flipping through an appointment book. "Today is Monday..."

My God! Bart was suddenly hit with the full realization of it. This *was* Monday. Three weeks exactly. That's when it had all started, when his world, so comfortable, safe, predictable, had begun to unravel. Could so much ruin have been inflicted upon it in so short a time?

"What about ten-thirty Wednesday morning?" Dr. Bissett pressed on. "Would that be satisfactory?"

"Sure," Bart answered absently. "Anything you say."

"Good! We'll see each other then,...and continue our little chat. I'll be interested in knowing how you've been getting along. All right?"

Bart experienced no noticeable effect from the pill, neither that one nor the others that he took, as instructed, every four hours throughout the remainder of the day. He had rather looked forward to a respite of some kind, once he knew what they were, and when none came, it crossed his mind that the good doctor had perhaps been toying with him, giving him a placebo, just to see what happened.

He knew that if he went directly home at five o'clock, the temptation would be there to have a drink, especially if the rat should start to give him any trouble. And so, despite his doubts about the pills, he stayed at the office, cleaning up work that should have been done during the day, while he was otherwise occupied. Then he followed through by eating supper in the Midtown area and taking in a movie afterward. It was past ten when he arrived at the house, too late to do anything about the traps. They would have to wait till morning at the earliest.

Bart experienced an exceptionally virulent case of the jitters in passing through the door under the stoop and subsequently in climbing to his third-floor bedroom/bathroom compound. He combated it by turning on every light in the house as he proceeded. It worked relatively well, that is, until he reached his destination. There, he was accosted by a strong premonition. Something was terribly wrong in his bedroom. He made himself open the door in spite of it.

Relying on the hall light to illuminate the way, he made for the bedside table nearest him, cautiously looking all about him as he proceeded. There he reached over and flicked on the lamp.

"Oh, good God! NO!"

His bed was littered with rat droppings.

Bart stormed about the room, tearing it apart, ranting and raving. Nothing was overlooked. Books were thrown to the floor from bookcases, the draperies wrenched and shaken, almost ripped down to see behind, the mattress upended, drawers yanked open and their contents spilled. When he was finished, the room was in chaos and Bart stood in the middle of it like a mad giant, breathing heavily, still searching, wild-eyed, heart and head pounding.

She was nowhere in the room, nor had he uncovered a clue as to how she had penetrated his defenses and gained access to his fortress.

Then, suddenly, he remembered. The heavy art books, which he had relied on to block the hole surrounding the radiator pipe, had been shoved aside, not much, just enough for her to pass.

"God *DAMN* you!" he shouted down to her, through the opening, banging the heavy brass handle of the poker against the side of the radiator in full fury. If she was anywhere near, it must have sounded to her like being at the bottom of an empty oil drum, while somebody pounded on the outside with a hammer. "GOD DAMN YOU, DO YOU HEAR ME?"

TWELVE

"COME OUT OF THERE AND FIGHT...OUT IN THE OPEN...YOU LOUSY YELLOW COWARD!" Bart continued railing at her. He was close to tears and shaking uncontrollably with anger and frustration over his impotence. But, of course, she paid him no mind, maintaining her distance and her silence, leaving him to ponder not only her whereabouts but also his mental stability.

To prevent himself from dwelling on either, he raised the bottle of scotch to his lips and poured, swallowed twice and wiped off the excess with the back of his hand. Then he went to work putting the room back into some sort of order. Adding more heavy art books to the original stack, he jammed these in so firmly they came close to lifting the radiator off its feet. There would be no shoving them aside another time.

He was winding up when it slammed into him out of nowhere. All of a sudden, the room started to spin crazily. Bart had the impression of being caught up in a rock slide and free-falling along with it, bounding, bouncing, tumbling. His eyes felt too big for their sockets and lost all ability to focus, his legs turned to jelly, the ground kept moving out from under him with each step he took. He was terribly dizzy, lurching, flapping his arms to catch something with which to steady himself, thought he would fall for certain.

As best he could, he wobbled toward his bed, couldn't make it, crumbled to the floor by its side. With all the willpower at his command, he grabbed for the center of the mattress, bunching the sheet and matting into a makeshift handle for his rubbery fingers, hauled himself to where he could swing his legs, one at a time, over the side of the bed and collapsed onto it.

Bart lost all sense of time or place.

Somewhere, he heard the rat digging. It was unhurried, but dogged as always. He desperately wanted to get up and give chase. But, for some reason, his muscles would not respond, however much he strained. Even his head felt too heavy to lift off the pillow. What was wrong with him? The sum total of what he *could* accomplish was a slow-motion roll of his head and eyes in the direction of the gnawing.

She was trying to dig her way through the art books. They were Meg's cherished possessions, rare, painstakingly collected over the years. She would be outraged to find them ruined. He never should have used them to block the hole. Stupid of him. Yet there had been nothing else at hand.

From the sound of it, the rat could not have far to go. The grinding stopped. Silence. Bart realized she had made it. Again, he grunted and groaned and strove to move, but he was as good as paralyzed from the neck down.

He watched her stick her nose out. It and her long black whiskers twitched excitedly and her beady eyes sparkled, as she sniffed out her bearings. She stole a few more furtive steps into the room, took another reading, spotted him lying on the bed. She must have sensed that he was also helpless, for she started to squeal with delight and anticipation.

Instinctively, Bart tried to cry out for help, but only his mouth moved. No voice came with it.

Satisfied there was no present danger separating her from her objective, the rat scuttled across the dark green carpet, as far as the bedside table. There, she paused, looking, listening, smelling.

Again, Bart labored mightily to call out, or at least to issue some sound that might distract her, if not in fact provoke her into flight. The best he could summon was a guttural rattle.

She was not impressed, holding her ground by the side of the bed, making sure to keep herself plainly within his field of vision, softening him up, while she mulled her options.

Again, he struggled to rise, but it was no go. He was immobilized as securely as had he been literally strapped there, arms, legs and trunk. What *had* happened to him?

All at once, without advance signal, the rat sprang into action, tearing up the side of the headboard, onto the top ledge, coming to a halt directly above his vulnerable, upturned face. Defensively, simultaneously, he clamped his eyes shut. Maybe, just maybe, if they were not open for her to notice, she would not be tempted by them.

They darted about in the darkness behind his eyelids, the same as if open and searching for her, in an effort to divine when and where she would make her next move. But it did not materialize. His facial muscles around the eyes were tiring rapidly, as a consequence of his having to squeeze them so protectively. They were beginning to quiver, out of control.

He knew he mustn't, but the temptation was too strong, his curiosity too great. Tentatively, guardedly, he relaxed the muscles concerned, allowed his eyes to open into narrow slits. Through the meshing eyelashes, he could vaguely make out her dark and menacing presence, perched on the ledge, studying him intently, her sides expanding and contracting evenly. They showed not the slightest evidence of her being out of breath, despite her considerable exertion and the excitement of the moment.

Bart worked at curbing them, but his eyelids would not cooperate. They were being pulled open as resistlessly as though drawn by magnets. The more he saw of her, the more he *had* to see of her.

She stood fast, motionless, never taking her eyes off him. They were cruel and full of hate and held his under their hypnotic spell, open as wide as saucers.

She stepped off the ledge.

Time stood still for him, as he watched her drop, almost float, toward his unprotected face. Her eyes continued to hold his to hers, and her mouth was open, the upper lip curled back, exposing her two razor-sharp incisors pointing straight down in readiness. Her long bony fingers were spread wide apart, their claws extended, set to go, while her skinny, scaly tail trailed behind her like that of a falling kite. Bart waited, transfixed, helpless.

A split second before she was to make a perfect four-point landing, he was inexplicably seized with the strength and will of a madman, intent on bursting his bonds. He exploded from his trance, spun to the right, fell off the bed, crashed to the floor. Instantaneously, he sprang to his feet with as automatic a reflex as that of a prizefighter after knockdown. He stood rooted to where he was, weaving unpredictably, dazed, disoriented, yet withal ready and willing to resume the clash.

But she was not on the bed.

Quickly, he reached down to pick up the poker which he spotted lying on the floor near the radiator. Too quickly, as it happened. His head started to pound and to twirl madly, he saw stars, straightened, regained his equilibrium in the nick of time.

Bart tried again, keeping his head level, moving more circumspectly, gingerly lowering himself to one knee, then to the other. Even in his hazy mental condition, he was most anxious to find out just how large a hole the rat had dug and, therefore, the extent of the damage to Meg's prized books.

In fact, there was neither.

Bart had dreamt the entire episode, and Dr. Bissett had been given the last laugh.

Relieved, disappointed, still groggy, Bart stood up. The lower half of the casement window was down. He relied on it now to lean out the window, using it to support his forearms, resting his chin on his folded hands. He was surprised to see how many of his apartment neighbors had their lights burning, imagined what night goblins they, too, were having to battle.

The first hints of the new day were emerging, the sky gradually exchanging its midnight blue for a friendlier pastel shade, the cool of the night giving way to the early hints of another scorching day. Around about, high up in the trees, the birds were tentatively twittering, identifying themselves, signaling to each other that they had made it through another perilous night. And slowly, the rumble of city traffic, silenced for a few hours, was building, soon to become the inevitable morning bumper-to-bumper chaos. Bart could only wonder what further woe this day held for him also.

He returned to his bed, knelt down beside it. He had

not said his prayers in years. There had been no time and, besides, things had been going well for him. He had not felt the need. But he did now.

Eliot Riverton's nine-thirty meeting was by this time only a few hours off. Bart was in no shape, physically or mentally, to take part in it, yet he thought it would not be politic for him to miss it. And so, he rested as best he could, short of falling asleep, until it was time to go. Still feeling too shaky to risk either the subway or the long walk, he took a taxi to get there.

Throughout the meeting, he could not get his mind off the rat, this in addition to his abiding, physical discomfort. He was caught off guard repeatedly, forced into answering questions without sufficient prior consideration, sometimes curtly, flippantly, giving the appearance of being unprepared, unprofessional and certainly unqualified to handle the investment burdens of such an important account

The ordeal was endless and excruciating for everyone concerned, and when Riverton left abruptly at the end, without comment to Bart, it was evident who he was holding answerable for the apparent loss of this major piece of new business.

It was noon before the cobwebs had cleared for good and Bart felt anything approaching his normal self. It was also then when it occurred to him that, except for her insolent and deliberately provocative defecation on his bed, he had not, in fact, heard anything from the rat in well over twenty-four hours. And, significantly, this period embraced that crucial nocturnal stretch which was routinely her busiest.

Had he been so stupefied by drink and pills as to hear nothing while he slept, or could God have anticipated his prayers and been granting them even as he knelt?

Whichever, there could be no mistaking the smell that accosted him when he arrived home that evening, particularly as he pushed open the door under the stoop. And it grew more fetid the further he proceeded into the house, through the kitchen, down the playroom stairs, to the barn-red fire door. It was all he could do to make himself turn the knob.

The stench of decomposition that exploded in his face when he did was more than he could bear, and he staggered, stumbled back into the playroom, gagging, gasping, pulling the knob with him, slamming the door shut as fast as he could. He hurtled up the stairs, coughing, snorting, taking two and three steps at a time. The odor followed him like a vapor trail, clinging to his nostrils as if it were a coat of paint, permeating his clothing, his skin.

Bart threw open the Dutch door, ran into the garden, breathed in deeply. Again. Again. Gradually the fetor wore off, little by little he recouped. He sat down at the glass-topped table to contemplate this unforeseen, yet welcome, sudden turn of events, and how best to deal with it.

So, the rat was dead. The poisoned meat had obviously worked the trick. Bart wished he had thought of it sooner. How much grief, how many sleepless nights could have been avoided.

He wondered how badly she had suffered, whether it was anywhere near enough to compensate for the anguish she had put him through. He pictured her in her death throes, writhing, convulsing, frothing, gurgling and begging the Almighty for release from the unendurable agony of the arsenic in her gut.

And yet, with that certain largesse reserved for the victorious, he was not without pity for the vanquished as well. After all, she had only done what was in her nature to do and, subsequently, what any self-respecting mother would feel like doing to the murderer of her children. She had pursued her purpose imaginatively and gallantly, using her strengths to their fullest extent and capitalizing on his every mistake and miscalculation, while keeping her own to the absolute minimum.

She had been a formidable adversary and merited a more dignified end. Indeed, based on relative performance, she probably should have won. But she hadn't and that was that. No one ever claimed life was fair. Why should death be? So be it.

Bart made ready for the burial. He decided on a snow shovel as the best means of transporting the remains. He triple-folded a heavy dishtowel and tied it across his nose and mouth. Lastly, he found an economy-size aerosol can of disinfectant spray in the cleaning supplies cabinet under the sink. He was as ready as he would ever be and set off.

The thick spray of disinfectant cleared a path for him, and breathing as much as he could through his mouth also helped. He experienced the same reluctance as earlier at the fire door, but made himself go through with opening it again, proceeding directly to the string dangling from the overhead light fixture. Without delay, he began the search.

He did not have far to look, but it was not the rat's rotting corpse that he found. It was the raw hamburger, on the floor, within a few feet of the doorway. Two days in that torrid, airless cellar had turned it dark gray, almost black, and it was covered with a grayish-greenish mold. Half of it had been eaten away and so had the bait from the seven traps. In some cases, even the string holding it had been likewise devoured.

The plastic ice cream container lay on its side, its contents of sugar and poison spilled and showing extensive evidence of the rat's keen interest in it. How much she might actually have consumed, however, was difficult to tell. But not so the pith helmet nearby. Its wide brim had been extensively gnawed into, presumably to get at its cork innards under the khaki cloth covering. One more thing of sentimental value had been destroyed.

Bart knew better than to indulge either his anger or his disappointment, or to dawdle in idle speculation as to just how effective the poison she had ingested had been. Until proven otherwise, he must assume that she was at most weak and ailing, but still capable of posing a very real and present danger.

He wrapped everything, including the oozing meat, in the brown paper bag, closed the door and hurried upstairs. Within a half hour, he was back at the fire door with a new batch of poisoned sugar and the seven traps cleaned and loaded. He planned to cock them in the playroom. This would cut to the bone the amount of time he would have to spend in the cellar itself.

One by one, he carried his explosive cargo to its predetermined place, opening and closing the door after each sally. He was determined to take no unnecessary chances. But the trips were nonetheless long, hellish and wearing in the extreme. He worried where to put his feet, lest he trip and fall over the piles of renovation material, scattered so senselessly around the room. He worried about the traps which he had cocked with all the delicacy and precision his long experience had taught him. The slightest misstep could cause one to detonate prematurely, doing untold harm to the fingers holding it.

But as always, what bothered him most was the feeling of her silently watching everything he was doing. He wondered if she was laughing at him now with his damn-fool traps which she knew all about. Curious how he had never been able to figure out where she actually made her home, although he had never doubted it was somewhere in that cellar.

After the fourth journey, he took a respite by shifting to spreading the poisoned sugar. It was still guesswork, at best, where to sprinkle it, but he concentrated as before along the base of walls, which he still considered her major travel arteries.

With the end in sight, his spirits were on the rise, although he was by no means letting down his guard. Back to the traps. Another placed, then another. One to go. Bart wished he had done this one first, rather than saving it for last. It was the trickiest, calling for slipping it down through a narrow passageway between some doors and the wall against which they were stacked.

Bart took a deep breath, reached for the trap. His hand had started to shake uncontrollably. He decided to wait, to give himself a chance to calm down, checking every now and again to see if the quivering was subsiding. Soon, he could delay no more.

Slowly, he stood up, holding the trap respectfully between his thumb and the second and third fingers, never removing his eyes from his fluttering payload. "Stop that!" he commanded his right hand impatiently, halfway to his goal. But the more he wanted it to, the more severe the affliction became, the same as when walking with an overfilled cup, carrying it by its saucer.

Suddenly, the dollhouse caught his eye or, more exactly, his fancy. This was one location he had not tried, and all the others he had, hadn't worked. Let's do it, he thought with a wry smile. Besides, it was closer; he could get rid of his hazardous load that much quicker.

Unlike most dollhouses whose backsides are permanently open, when Bart had built this one, he had included a rear panel. It was attached to the roof by three small hinges and could be swung up like a giant flap until every room on every floor was in plain view and easily accessible. When closed, the house had a more authentic look to it and could be seen into only through its windows and front door.

Cautiously, Bart detoured over toward it now, uneasily checking each next step before taking it. It was an unfamiliar route and the last thing he wanted was to stumble.

Safely there, he glanced quickly at the trap to check that all was as it should be and, at the same time, took in the area surrounding the house. He would have to be careful. The stuff piled irregularly all about created innumerable booby traps, any one of which could snag the trap while his eyes were diverted elsewhere.

Slowly he lowered himself, carefully starting to reach for the small brass handle near the bottom of the panel. It was the only externally visible sign that it could be raised. Again, he checked the trap. All was well. He let himself drop a little further.

His legs were getting tired, beginning to twitch nervously. He tried squeezing the muscles, hoping it would stop the shaking. No good. Never mind. Almost there. Good enough.

As he began lifting the panel, he glanced anxiously back and forth between it in his left hand and the trap in his right. Everything was in order, proceeding nicely.

All of a sudden, there was frenzied activity inside the house. The rat bolted out the front door. Horrified, Bart let go, toppling backward. The panel slammed down with a resounding, hollow thud. Tiny white feathers, identical to those that had littered the linen closet floor, puffed out the open windows. Bart scarcely had time to notice.

Devastating pain had shot into his hand, through the

wrist, into the elbow. Spots swirled before his eyes, his stomach was in his throat. The rat trap was clamped onto his second and third fingers, just beyond their first knuckles. He blacked out.

Bart had no idea how long he'd been unconscious when he came to. He was sprawled on the floor. The rat was nowhere to be seen. Desperately he struggled to rise, frantically trying to pry the spring off his throbbing fingers. He was whimpering in pain, close to hysteria.

"Oh, God!" he cried out in his grief.

The rat squealed with delight, the same as the night she had attacked him in his bed. By the sound, she was near the furnace, must have been under it He could not see her. She squealed again gleefully.

"Oh, Jesus!" Bart moaned, stumbling, lurching toward the open fire door.

"Now's your chance, goddam you!" he bellowed at her over his shoulder, continuing to stagger ahead, not watching, not caring where he put his feet.

His legs and ankles were rubbery and the pain in his fingers remorseless. Maybe it would be better if the rat did attack him, put an end to it all. He didn't care about that either.

Instinctively, he reached for the door as he passed, giving it an automatic tug, but it would not budge. To hell with it! What difference had it made being closed, anyway?

Bart zigzagged up the stairs, clutching the banister as both support and hoist. The trap hung on his fingers like the weight on a plum line. In his entire life, never had he experienced agony the like of it.

Propping himself against the kitchen sink, he thrust trap and fingers both under the cold-water spigot. Instantly, some relief, not much, but some. Thank God.

The ends of his fingers had turned an ominous deep

purple. Every action to extricate them seemed only to intensify the distress. The spring was slippery, intractable and utterly without pity. Twice he had his fingers almost free, twice he lost control of the spring. It smashed back down on them, causing further excruciating pain, a wave of nausea and spots before his eyes.

At last, they were clear. The trap dropped into the basin. The cold water washed his blood from it.

Gratefully, Bart slumped against the counter, continuing to hold his fingers under the cooling, soothing flow. Gradually, they regained some of their normal color, although clearly, they had been badly injured.

When he felt equal to it, he wrapped his hand in ice and a Turkish towel and headed for the Emergency Room of the hospital three blocks from his house. He figured his fingers were more than likely fractured and that, in any case, someone who would know should have a look at them.

It was well before the nighttime rush hour for a city hospital emergency room, and Bart was therefore taken care of promptly. X-rays were made, a splint for both fingers strapped on and a prescription for codeine written out.

"Well, sir, how are you feeling now?" the doctor asked, reentering Bart's cubicle, nearing the examining table he had been taken to on his arrival. This was Bart's first real chance to look at him objectively. He was outfitted in the same green material as the divider curtains and it struck Bart that they must be graduating doctors younger these days.

"Slightly beat, I'll have to admit," Bart said, sounding it. "But at least you got this goddam hand to stop hurting the way it did. Jesus! I've never known anything like it."

"You were very, very lucky," the doctor said, looking

down at Bart's bandaged hand resting on his chest. "No breaks, not even a hairline fracture. That's very unusual for an accident of this kind, I'd say."

"Oh?"

"People don't understand how vicious car doors can be. Take them for granted. Why, we've had patients come in here with fingers virtually sheared right off by them."

"Jesus! Makes me hurt more just to hear about it."

The car-door ploy was something Bart had concocted en route to the hospital. There was no reason in the world he shouldn't have told this young doctor the truth, except that he really didn't have the strength to go into the whole ghastly saga.

"You'll be good as new in a couple of days, but when the novocaine wears off, it's likely to hit you pretty hard. So, you'd best be taking it a little easy, tomorrow anyway, preferably in bed. Besides, you'll...Have you had much previous experience with codeine?"

"Not to speak of. I'm not sure I've ever taken any."

"Well, I think you'll find that it makes you kind of drowsy. You won't be feeling much like going any fifteen rounds with Muhammad Ali, or anything of that kind," he said, smiling reassuringly. "And while you're at it, stay away from car doors, too, for a while. Okay?" He turned to leave.

"Uh...Doctor!" Bart called, suddenly filled with remorse for having lied to him, wanting to rectify it. More to the point, he was also seized by an overwhelming urge to talk with someone, and this doctor struck him as the kind who would understand, with or without firsthand experience.

"Yes?"

"Say...uh...uh...thanks a lot!" Bart retreated, losing his nerve.

"Anytime," the doctor replied, holding his eyes on him that extra second too long, as if sensing Bart's midstream change of course. "Anytime," he repeated, pushed the green curtain aside and was gone.

"Feel strong enough to get up?" the nurse asked, taking over almost simultaneously.

"Sure," Bart faked with a wan smile, wishing he could stay. He swung his legs over the side of the examining table, started to get up. The blood drained from his head.

"There's nothing to rush about," she said gently, holding him by his good arm. Gradually he and the room settled down.

"How long would you like me to wear this thing?" Bart asked, examining the arm sling she was adjusting around his neck.

"That'll be pretty much up to you. It's just to ease the throbbing. You'll know when you don't need it any more. Would you like us to try and call you a cab?"

"No. No, thanks. That's okay. I live only three blocks up the street. The walk'll do me good."

"You sure, now?"

"Sure."

In fact, the walk did just that. Getting his mind off his troubles, even for a little while, seemed to revitalize him. He filled the codeine prescription at his regular drugstore on Second Avenue, relying on the same car-door ruse to keep the pharmacist's inquisitiveness at bay, and continued to the corner delicatessen.

"Hey! What'd you go and do to yourself, my friend?" the proprietor asked.

"Smashed my fingers. Just coming from the hospital, matter of fact, getting fixed up."

"That's a damn shame. How'd it happen?"

"Car door," Bart answered quickly. It came easier with each use. "Nice people down there."

Much as he might have felt like opening up with the doctor in the Emergency Room, he viewed it now as having been a temporary lapse, a moment of weakness. The rat was no one's business but his, and he intended to keep it that way.

"So I've heard tell," the proprietor said. "Man! It's sure been one lousy summer for you, eh? I mean, first off that business with the rat and now this coming right on top of it."

"Yes, I know."

"Well, maybe that'll be your fill of bad luck for a while."

"I hope so."

"Speaking of which, you never did tell me what finally became of that rat. How did that turn out?"

"Dead," Bart said matter of factly.

"That so?"

"Yup!"

"That's great! Congratulations! How'd it happen?"

"Trap," Bart said absently, pretending consuming interest in several of the counter displays.

"When?"

"Oh, let's see. I've kind of lost track by now...uh...yes, that's it. Thursday. Last Thursday."

"No kidding. Some relief, eh?"

"You know it. To tell the truth, I'm not sure how much more of that rat I could've stood."

"I can believe it." The proprietor was ringing Bart's purchases into the cash register. "Funny thing, though."

"What's that?"

"Thursday, you say?"

"That's right."

"I could've sworn...but it can't be. Didn't I see you in here just the other day? Sunday, I think it was?"

"Yes, that's right. I was in here Sunday," Bart confirmed confidently. "What about it?"

"Yeah, that's what I thought. Oh, nothing much...it's only that I could swear I sold you another box of poison that day...no?" He looked genuinely perplexed.

"No!" Bart snapped defensively, before he could catch himself. "You must be mistaking me for someone else," he said to soften it.

"Yeah, that must be it. Still...funny...I can't seem to get it out of my head..."

"Yes, well, see you around," Bart said hastily, grabbing the bag of groceries with his good left arm.

"Crazy, isn't it?"

"What?" Bart asked from the door.

"I mean, the tricks your mind plays on you sometimes."

THIRTEEN

Bart wasted no time in getting home. He wished he hadn't lied like that. But it wasn't his fault. Not really. The delicatessen proprietor had no business prying, asking all those questions. They might have sounded innocent enough on the surface, but Bart was no fool. He knew better. Damn the man, anyway!

It was awkward having to do everything with his left hand, starting with the front door key, which was buried deep down in his right trouser pocket. Bart contorted, stretched, pulled, cursed, all to no avail. His arm in the. sling kept getting in the way, and the key eluded his grasp. He was contemplating abandoning the effort in favor of a passing stranger, and was actually debating which would be preferable, a man or woman, when he succeeded.

He moved as fast as he could in the circumstances, proceeding immediately to his bedroom/bathroom fortress, closing the door behind him and clicking its push-button lock into position. He deposited the bag of groceries on the desk, tossed the poker onto the bed, took his first codeine pill and began the laborious task of getting out of his clothes.

As the doctor had forewarned, the novocaine wore off, with a vengeance. It was as though all the pain it had been anesthetizing had been held in storage, accumulating, pending eventual release in one great surge.

Bart leaped out of bed, ripped away the sling, clutching his hand by the wrist, squeezing, massaging, rubbing the back of it, coming as close as he dared to the injured fingers, pumping his arm up and down. The pain radiated well into his shoulder joint. He paced the floor, moaning, and damning the codeine for being so ineffective. He knew he shouldn't; it was too soon after the first one, but the pain drove him to it. He downed another pill. Within a half hour or so, the fingers eased, and he was able to doze off.

Bart was somewhere by the sea, sitting on the dunes. He did not recognize the place. It looked like everywhere but nowhere, too. The sun was at its noonday brightest. He was sweating. A swim would surely be marvelous. Someone suggested it. People all around jumped excitedly to their feet and ran gaily to the water's edge, shouting, laughing, exulting at the prospect. Then, Bart remembered. His hand. Slammed the fingers in a car door. See the bandage? The doctor said above all not to get it wet.

The telephone began to ring and he ran back to the house to answer it. He was struck by how much it resembled the dollhouse, wondered if he had built this one, too. His hand was in his pocket. He couldn't get it out. It made running difficult. The pressure against it made it hurt, throb. Finally, he wrenched it free. Better. The telephone rang and rang, and he ran and ran to get to it in time. But he couldn't find it anywhere. Goddammit! Somebody had misplaced it. Oh, there it was. Too late. Only the dial tone in the receiver.

In the distance, the sound of sawing echoing through the woods, trees being felled. He thought it could be the Black Forest. Same dankness, the sun hardly able to break the dense green cover. Was that his friends he heard still frolicking in the surf? Too cold in the forest for swimming. He hadn't realized before how near to the sea it was.

Little waves lapped at the door of the house, too. And he could distinguish gnawing there as well. Be through soon, whatever it was. No time to waste. Must get at it. He threw open the door, in hot pursuit.

It had to be her.

Bart was wearing only his eyeglasses. Not the optimum combat uniform. Frantically, he started searching for his hunting clothes. Where *were* they, goddammit? Had Meg put them away somewhere? Damn! Damn! What right did she have to do that? The rat was none of her business. Nobody's. Found them. On the bed. What the *hell* were they doing there? No time now to worry about it.

The trousers were bundled into a ball. They felt heavier than usual for some reason. Bart shook out the legs. The rat plopped onto the floor. The same sound as a man's bare fist smashing into another's face. Disgusting! That's right. Rats *are* disgusting. Everything about them. Cletus had said so.

But what were all those tiny white feathers everywhere? Of course! Her nest. That's what it was. Bart had discovered where she lived at last. Clete had said that was important to know, too.

There was something the matter with her tail. It looked almost severed, as if hanging on by no more than a little skin. Served her right! He wondered how she had done it. It didn't seem to hurt her much, though, or lessen her speed and mobility to any marked degree.

She disappeared.

"Where are you, goddam your rotten soul? Come out!"

He was shouting at the top of his lungs. Why didn't she answer him?

Dejectedly, he sat down on a wooden crate nearby. He could hear his friends still cavorting happily in the waves. And those people in the forest They were still at it, too. Grind. Grind. Who could they be?

"My God! What are you doing? Those are my fingers you're sawing." But they paid no heed. Grind. Grind.

"Stop! Stop! Are you people crazy, for Christ's sake? Stop! Stop! I can't stand it any-more. Stop!"

More and more and more, the grief in his fingers built, but nothing he could do or say would make them stop. And the awful sound their sawing made. Grind. Grind. Bart thought he would go mad if they didn't stop soon. They had to. Had to.

He woke up.

Time for another pill.

Thus, the long night hours crept by for him, in and out of sleep, in and out of reality, in and out of varying degrees of suffering. But there was this much to say for it. The rat did not take advantage of the situation, letting him be, forsaking her customary nightly harassment. He was at a loss to explain it, only profoundly grateful for it, and to her.

It was eight-twenty Wednesday morning when the telephone startled him to life. Groggily, he stumbled for the desk, automatically reaching for the receiver with his right hand. In his haste to get there before it stopped ringing, he smacked his injured fingers hard into it. The receiver rolled out of its cradle and fell to the desk top.

"Unh-h-h-oh-h-h! Jesus!" Bart reacted, recovering it with his left hand.

"Hey! Are you all right?" came the voice from the other end.

"I...I think so," Bart stammered between gasps. He shifted the receiver to his right side, cradling it between his ear and shoulder, massaged his right hand with his left. "Who...who is this, anyway?"

"WHO is this, in a pig's eye! It's none other than your friendly, faithful, reliable, last of the good guys, real estate agent. That's WHO this is."

"Oh, Jesus, Phil. Not now. I'm just not up to it. And what are you doing calling me so early in the morning?" his speech thick and lifeless.

Phil Lavin made a specialty of working with brownstones on the Upper Eastside. Bart considered him rather a nuisance with his quarterly letters and repeated phone calls, promising untold riches from unnamed third parties who had eyes for his house and his only. But the fact remained that he had indeed moved several on Bart's block at prices which made even their ecstatic owners blush. And so, over the years, Bart had put up with the rest in order to stay in his good graces. As he had once put it to a questioning Meg, "You never know when we're going to want to sell this place, and when we do, there's no one, but no one, who can do it the way Phil Lavin can."

"So EARLY?" Phil protested. "Hell! I've been at work for hours already."

"Oh," Bart allowed noncommittally, still emerging from the abyss. Besides, this was standard patter with Phil, claims of ceaseless overwork.

"Like I keep trying to get you to appreciate, as long as there are rich guys to work for, there's going to be no R and R for the rest of us poor working slobs."

"Yes, you have made that point once or twice before," Bart observed coolly. He never liked it when people made reference, however obliquely, to his privileged background. He considered it a put-down which, as often as not, was the precise intent. "Look, Phil, I'm not feeling at all well…"

"No sweat," Phil interrupted. "This'll just take a minute, then I'll let you go back to your beauty rest. I tried you last night, as a matter of fact."

"You did? When?"

"Must have been around nine-thirty, ten, something like that. I let the phone ring and ring, figuring if you were there, it could take you a while to get to it…the place is so damn big…and if you weren't, what the hell? Gave me a chance to rest," he said with an appreciative chuckle.

Vaguely Bart could recall something about a telephone ringing and a house somewhere and his running for it, only to have it fall silent as he reached it. "So that was you?" he said softly, mysteriously, to himself essentially.

"You mean you were there?" Phil asked, overhearing, sounding annoyed.

"No. No. I was thinking about something else. Sorry."

The give and take was good therapy for Bart's fingers. They were recovering quickly from their collision with the receiver.

"Hey, no problem. No apologies needed, none asked for. This is your old buddy, Phil, you got here on the pipe."

"Appreciate it, Phil…but, look, I don't mean to come across as rude or…"

"Like I said. It'll only take a minute. I've got a proposition for you. It's too sweet to pass up and I just *had* to walk it past you."

"Phil," Bart broke in wearily, "Meg and I aren't interested in selling the place right now and so…"

"Not even for fifty G's more than you told me you've

got in that house?" he said deliberately, enunciating every word.

"That sounds pretty good, I must admit, Phil, but..."

"PRETTY GOOD! Why, it's absolutely nothing short of fantastic. FAN...TAS...TIC! That's what I told these people the place was worth and they didn't bat an eye...not an eye. When your old buddy-boy, Phil, says he's got a deal that's too sweet to pass up, you can bet your bottom dollar that's just what he's got."

"Yes, I realize that, Phil, and I appreciate your walking it past me. Really, I do. But, I'm just not ready. Meg's away...and, as I said to you, I'm feeling like hell..."

"Yeah, you did say that. What's the matter with you, anyhow? Hope nothing too serious. But, like I was telling you before, there's fifty big ones out there, just waiting for the taking. Can you picture the home you and Meg could move into with all that scratch put together in one beautiful bundle? Come to think of it, I've got just the place for you, I mean, when you're ready."

The easing in Bart's fingers proved illusory. They were starting to act up again. Time for another pill. And he was hungry as well. He wished Phil would go away.

"No, Phil. And that's final. The timing's off. I'm just not in the mood to move right now, I guess."

"Hey! Don't be getting me wrong. I'm not saying you should go out and sell right now. Nossir! All I'm asking is you to let me bring these people around, show them the place. That's all. Honest. How about it?"

"Really, Phil, there's no point...uh..."

Bart had been rummaging in the grocery bag on the desk with his left hand, dividing his attention between that and fending off Phil. He found the box of Fig Newtons he wanted.

"What can it hurt?" Phil pressed.

"Oh, no!" Bart exclaimed, horrified, letting go the box.

"What happened?" Phil demanded.

Bart spread open the bag, looked down into it.

"Aw, shit!" He inadvertently relaxed his right shoulder. The receiver dropped from its notch like a stone, clanking loudly on the bare wooden desk top.

"Hey! Will you tell me what's going on over there?" called the voice from it.

Bart's decision was made.

"When?" he said, picking up the receiver.

"When what?"

"When do you want to bring these people around?"

"You serious?"

"Just tell me when."

"Friday."

"What time?"

"Two-thirty...leastways, that's what I told them...I mean, pending your OK, of course."

"Fine. Two-thirty Friday it is. Meet you here."

"You sure? I mean, why the sudden about-face?"

"Phil. Suit yourself. Do you or don't you...?" 'We'll be there."

"Good!" Bart said, hanging up, disgustedly throwing the bag of groceries out the bedroom window.

FOURTEEN

At last. At last. At last. Bart could see light at the end of the tunnel. It wasn't the solution he would have preferred, but he recognized it now as the answer to his prayers. The ways of the Lord are mysterious indeed and most often best left unquestioned.

Shortly past ten-forty, the telephone rang again. Bart had been dozing lightly from the effects of the codeine pill he had taken right after Phil Lavin's call.

"Well, hello, there!" the caller greeted Bart cheerily. "I was under the impression you and I kind of had a date this morning."

"Oh, hi, Dr. Bissett," Bart said groggily. "Damn! That's right. I'm so sorry. I guess it sort of got away from me."

"Yes, of course. Nothing to be upset about. My loss, I'd say." He laughed hollowly. "Anyway, I tried your office first and...uh...no one seemed to know exactly where you were today. I understand your secretary is out, too, feeling a bit under the weather." This was news to Bart, for he had also forgotten to notify his office that he'd be spending the day at home. "Must be this summer flu bug that's been making the rounds," Dr. Bissett resumed. "Is this what has you down, too?"

"No, it isn't. I smashed my fingers in a car door yesterday."

"Oh, I'm sorry to hear that Nothing broken, I hope?"

"No, thank God. The doctor at the Emergency Room said I was really lucky."

"I should say so, too. Well, now. What say we try and reschedule our little talk? You aren't by any chance planning to come in this afternoon, are you?"

"I hadn't planned on it...but...uh...if you want me to, I can..."

"No. No. It's not that important. I was only thinking that if by chance...well, then, maybe we could work something out for tomorrow?"

"Oh, yes. I definitely plan on..."

"Splendid! Shall we say same time, same station?" Again, there was that hollow little laugh.

"Sure. You bet. That'd be fine with me," Bart answered. With his newly found elation had come a surge of confidence. Whereas he would have dreaded a meeting with Dr. Bissett before, and did, now he rather looked forward to it. He might even discuss the rat with him.

"And...uh, Dr. Bissett, again, I'm so sorry about today's foul-up."

"Please! There's no need. These things happen. We'll look for you in the morning, then."

Bart's euphoria carried him into the noon hour when his hunger pangs not only reasserted themselves but also got the better of him. He had put off responding to them earlier because he knew what a hassle it would be for him to get dressed. Also, the codeine pill had so dulled them that he forgot.

With the food he had bought at the delicatessen last

night lying splattered below in the garden and nothing else in the house, he would have to go out. Just as well. He was keen to get some fresh air anyway, and this was the first time he had felt up to it since returning from the hospital.

Bart recalled a Hamburger Heaven on Madison Avenue which he passed on his way to work. He wanted someplace far removed from his neighborhood, to lessen the chances of encountering anyone he or Meg might know. He was in no mood to deal with the inevitable prying into his private affairs, such as what had he done to his hand and why wasn't he at the office like every other self-respecting, up-and-coming bank officer.

After his meal Bart went to Carl Schurz Park and spent the afternoon there. It was rich in things to do and he did most of them: investigating the comings and goings at the Mayor's Mansion, inspecting the Senator Robert P. Wagner, Sr., fireboat, supervising the traffic plowing the river and bumper-to-bumper on the FDR Drive, watching the people, young and old, happy and sad, walking and jogging, the doers, the sitters, and the dogs. Time flew.

He ate supper out as well, took in a movie on Eighty-sixth Street and arrived home around nine-thirty. His hand had vastly improved and, all in all, given the circumstances, it had been a good day.

The rat was in the kitchen when he entered the house. He heard the scurrying, the scratching of her sharp claws on the bare tile floor, followed by tha-lump...tha-lump... tha-lump, down the playroom stairs. Bart detoured from his intended route only long enough to shut the door behind her and proceeded directly to his bedroom, locking himself in. If he was ineffective with two good hands, how could he expect to do battle with only one? He had reached that decision sitting in the park.

Before turning out the light, he took a codeine pill, not

that he needed it for pain necessarily, but mostly he thought it would help him get to sleep and keep him there. Lying on his bed in the dark, waiting for the drug to take effect, he was suddenly afflicted with outrage, the first he had felt since agreeing to Phil Lavin's proposition.

It was an outrage, and nothing short of it, to be forced by the rat to vacate the house he loved. But what could he do? He had reached the limit of his endurance, and in his soul, he knew now that he would never defeat her. The best he could hope for was a live-and-let-live kind of truce, but she would never be willing to grant him that, and even if she did, he could never trust her to keep her end of the bargain. No, he was beaten, and that was that.

But he was without shame. He had put up the best fight he knew how. Somebody had to win and somebody had to lose. He wished Phil and his clients were coming tomorrow instead of Friday. He fell asleep.

Throughout the night, she taunted him, daring *him* to come out and fight. She ran through the walls and ceiling, crashing about, gnawing, scratching, into the bathroom, behind the tub, tha-lump...tha-lumping outside his door, down the carpeted staircase, hour after hour. But Bart refused to rise to any of it, huddling under his bedsheet, waiting for this interminable night to end.

She kept after him until well after daybreak and when the alarm went off his total sleep could not have exceeded a couple of hours. He was exhausted and profoundly depressed. The euphoria of the previous day was gone and in its place was the nagging question, "What if they don't like the house, decide not to buy it?"

A few minutes before the appointed hour Thursday morning, Bart reluctantly pushed open the door with the frosted glass. The reception area was filled to capacity. Every eye turned on him as he entered, as if wanting to ascertain at a glance what ailment afflicted this latest arrival.

"Mr. Hughes?" the nurse behind the desk asked him pleasantly. Bart nodded. She must have been out or in another room on his first visit, although she did look familiar. Bart reckoned he had probably seen her in the bank cafeteria, but in any case, it was of no great importance.

"Yes, I thought you might be," she said. "Doctor is expecting you. Please go right in." He felt slightly guilty contributing further to the wait of those already there, but proceeded directly to where the nurse was pointing with her eyes. He knocked timorously on another door with frosted glass. This one said, "E. Forbes Bissett III, M.D." in bold gold letters across the center and "Examining Room" in smaller ones at the lower left. A sudden chill ran up Bart's spine. He sighed deeply, turned the knob.

"Yes?" came the voice from within. "Ah! It's you! Excellent!" Dr. Bissett welcomed him, glancing at his watch.

"I'm not late, am I?"

"Not at all. Right on time. It's nice to see you again, Bart."

"Nice to see you, too, Dr. Bissett," Bart lied, closing the door behind him.

"Sit down, won't you?" Dr. Bissett said, motioning him to the same little stool he had perched on before.

"Ever notice the funny little tricks your mind plays on you sometimes?" Bart asked by way of making conversation, but mostly to camouflage his acute uneasiness.

"Do you have an example?"

"Yes. That door there. I don't remember it being there when I was here the other day."

"Oh, it was there, all right. Only, it's kept open ..." most of the time." Bart didn't like the sound of that at all. "That's probably the reason you didn't notice it."

"Yes. Probably."

"The memory is an unpredictable instrument," Dr. Bissett closed the topic, folding back several sheets of his yellow pad, so as to have a fresh one to write on. "Be that as it may, how have you been getting along? The pills help?"

"Oh, yes. They were terrific. Slept like a log," Bart lied again. "But of course, I stopped taking them when I started with that other stuff."

"Other stuff?"

"Yes. You know. The codeine."

"Yes, I see." Dr. Bissett wrote the word "codeine" as the second entry on his yellow pad. The first had been Bart's name. "And what made you start taking codeine, if I may ask?"

"They gave it to me at the hospital...when I went there for my hand. I didn't think it would be a good idea to mix what you gave me with that, andso..."

"Oh, yes, of course. That was a very wise decision. And when exactly *did* you injure your hand?"

"When I got home after work...uh...last Tuesday."

"I see." Dr. Bissett wrote this down, too. "I didn't know you drove to work, Bart. That's rather unusual, I would say. Where do you find a place to park in this area?"

"I don't drive to work, Dr. Bissett."

"Forgive me, Bart. I guess when you told me you hurt your hand in a car door and that it was after work, I put two and two together...my mistake.... So what you're *really* telling me is that you're part of a car pool? That makes a great deal of sense, a car pool. Certainly preferable to that subway ride, I should say." Bart felt that Dr. Bissett was setting him up, for what he didn't know, but he didn't like it.

"I'm not *really* telling you anything, Dr. Bissett... except that I hurt my hand in a car door. That's what I'm *really* telling you and that's all that I'm *really* telling you."

"I apologize, Bart I didn't mean to upset you."

"And I'm NOT upset!"

"Yes, of course. You know Bart," Dr. Bissett said softly, "I can only be as helpful as you will allow me to be. Okay?"

"Yes. I'm sorry. I know you're just trying to do your job," Bart corrected himself. "I apologize."

"That's perfectly all right, Bart. You've been under a strain. I understand that. And so, you said you went to the hospital. The Emergency Room, I believe?"

"Yes. That's right. It's only three blocks from my house. I walked there," he volunteered as an indication of his willingness to be open and cooperative.

"You were lucky...I mean, to be so near a hospital where you could be taken care of...as well as so near your home like that." Dr. Bissett was writing while he spoke. Almost two-thirds of the legal-size page was already covered.

"Yes, I know. And they were really nice down there... especially the young doctor who took charge of my case. He was an Indian or a Pakistani...I can never tell the difference."

"Yes, I'm sure. Did he say anything was broken?"

"No. I mean, yes, he did say no, if you see what I'm saying." Bart laughed weakly. "He took a bunch of x-rays."

"Better to be safe than sorry, I'd say," the doctor replied, followed by that hollow little laugh.

"Christ, but it hurt! And then, I couldn't get the goddam thing to let go," Bart let slip.

"You mean the car door? That's what wouldn't let go? Wasn't there anybody inside who could open the door for you?"

Bart broke out in a cold sweat. He felt cornered. The room began to swim, he teetered on the little stool, blinked, tried to get hold of himself.

"I think I'm going to be sick," he said in a whisper.

Dr. Bissett helped him onto the examining table, broke open a small vial of something, waved it once or twice under his nose, something powerful. Bart jerked his head away.

"Ammonium carbonate," Dr. Bissett reassured him. "Some people call it smelling salts," he explained with a smile.

Bart felt better. The room stopped spinning, the ceiling lights lost their glare, his queasiness passed.

"Whew! That was close, Dr. Bissett. Thanks."

"You're very welcome, Bart. Your body has suffered a terrible shock, you know...slamming your fingers in a car door like that. It's bound to upset your whole system and take a goodly number of days until you're back to your old self."

"Oh-h-h-o-o-o, Christ! I'm so goddam tired."

"Yes, I can imagine. You just take it nice and easy for a little while," Dr. Bissett said soothingly. "There's no pressure on you now. No phone calls to be gotten to, no one riding you for this or that, nor pressing decisions to be made." While Bart rested, Dr. Bissett completed another sheet of his yellow pad, then, "Better?"

"Yes, thanks, Dr. Bissett. Sometimes I just don't know how much more I can take."

"I've suspected as much, Bart. But you'd be surprised how many there are just like you...in a large corporation... not just this one...any organization, I mean...so impersonal, brutal, really. There's no time for the little guy. And that's exactly why I'm here."

"No, you don't understand," Bart said earnestly.

"Oh, I understand perhaps a lot more than you think, Bart. But, as I was saying, this is where I see my most useful role...trying to help people cope."

"But, Dr. Bissett..."

"Now, just take it easy, Bart. Everything's going to be just fine. We're in this thing together...and..." Suddenly, Bart couldn't stand the pretense any longer, second only to Dr. Bissett's infernal prattle and bending everything to fit his preconceived notions.

"Goddammit, Dr. Bissett," Bart exploded, "a rat did this to me!"

"*Rattus Norvegicus* or *Homo sapiens?*" Dr. Bissett asked innocently, accompanied by another hollow little laugh.

"No, really. I mean it. The four-legged kind."

"A rat smashed your fingers? Is that what you're telling me, Bart?"

"No. Not exactly. But it was because of her. Actually, a trap did it...when the back of the doll-house dropped."

"The back of the dollhouse dropped, is that what you said, Bart?"

"Yes, that's right. And that's what made the trap go off."

"I see, Bart. So, it wasn't a car door, after all?"

"That's right."

"And it wasn't the rat that you mentioned, either...but a trap? Is that what you're saying?"

"Yes. Yes, that *is* what I'm saying."

"I see. And how long has this rat been bothering you?"

"Almost a month. I can remember exactly. It was at the

end of the Fourth of July weekend. She came into the house from the garden."

"I understand. So, you actually saw the rat come into the house? That must have given you quite a fright."

"I didn't see her exactly. It was really just a blur."

"I see. But you knew it was a rat, nonetheless?"

"Not right away. It wasn't until a week or ten days later, when she wrecked the clothes washer. I began to suspect it then."

"I see. And so, since that time...for the last month or so, as you say...you've been trying to catch this rat, or should I say, these rats?"

"Yes, that's right. I mean no. There's only one rat and, yes, I have been trying to catch her all this time."

"I see. I must confess to you, Bart, that must be *some* rat to elude capture for so long."

"You can say that again. She's something!"

"Yes. And I presume you've used poison and traps and things like that...things one would normally associate with killing a rat?"

"My God, yes! But she's too smart. She won't come near anything I put out for her."

"And where exactly *is* this rat?"

"In the house."

"Yes, I know. But what I had in mind was, could...or rather, can you be a little more specific?"

"I think mostly in the cellar. But she gets around the house with no trouble at all. She's wrecked stuff all over the place. The other night, she was in my room."

"Oh?"

"Yes, even though the doors were closed...and locked. I still don't know how in the hell she does it."

"I see."

"But I know she was there."

"And how do you know that?"

"She got into the bag of groceries I brought home from the delicatessen. Ate most of the box of Fig Newtons I had in there, plus some Saltines, an orange, or part of it anyway, and the same with a banana."

"That's quite an appetite, I would say. Uh..."

"Yes. That's why I can't keep any food in the house. She'd find it wherever I tried to hide it."

"Yes, of course. But to return to the bag of groceries for a moment...the one you brought home from the delicatessen. How did you react when you saw what had been done to the food?"

"I threw the bag out the window."

"I see, yes. With the food still in it?"

"Yes. Of course. It was no damn good to me...I mean, after she had contaminated it and everything."

"I understand. So, of course, you just threw it out the window...into the street, I suppose?"

"Yes, that's right. I mean, no. Into the garden, not the street. And, by the way, that wasn't the first time she came into my room like that, either."

"Oh?"

"No. But at least this time she didn't attack *me*...just the food."

"Bart, forgive me for interrupting you, but..." he was flipping back through several sheets of his yellow pad, running his finger down each page. "Ah, yes. Here we are. You keep referring to the rat as "she" and "her" and I was wondering what makes you so certain it's a female."

"That's easy. She had a litter of little rats."

"Yes. I see. So, from that...yes, that makes sense. And where was this litter?"

"In the cellar. I killed them."

"No one could blame you for that."

"But she does."

"Yes, of course. But, now, could we go back to...uh... you said she didn't attack you, just the food this time?"

"That's right."

"Am I to assume from that that there was a time before when she attacked you...personally, I mean?"

"Yes. It was after I had knocked off her kids and she was mad as hell at me for it, you know?"

"Yes. Yes. Do go on, please."

"So, that night, she jumped up on the bed and came after me. To tell the truth...it sounds crazy, I know...but she came after my tes ...I mean, my testicles."

"I see."

"Rats do that, you know. They go after the softest body parts first, and so naturally, when she started up the bed, I figured this was what she was after."

"Naturally."

"But it turned out she was more interested in my eyes."

"And how did you determine that?"

"She jumped for them."

"By 'jumped for them,' you mean she flew through the air?"

"Yes, exactly."

"And what did you do?"

"I threw my arm across my eyes and ducked. She went flying past me. I felt her go by and then her furry body brush my shoulder, as she dropped to the pillow."

"And have you had other encounters with the rat?"

"Oh, yes. Once, she lured me down into the cellar, and when I got there, she swished her tail at me."

"Swished her tail at you? Could you elaborate on that just a bit?"

"Sure. She was up in the ceiling and let her tail drop through an opening, near the wall."

"I see."

"And she just swished it back and forth at me."

"So, what did you do?"

"I took a swipe at it with the fireplace poker."

"With the fireplace poker?"

"Yes. I make it a point of never going into the cellar unarmed or without my hunting gear...well, almost never."

"And what, may I ask, does your 'hunting gear' consist of...I mean, besides the fireplace poker?"

"Well, there's a pair of heavy corduroy trousers. That's one part. And then, a thick wool shirt, hunting boots, and, of course, my pith helmet."

"You wear a *pith helmet* when you go into the cellar?"

"I did. Until she knocked it off my head and ruined it."

"She knocked your pith helmet off your head and then ruined it? You mean when it fell off your head, that's what ruined it?"

"No. No. She chewed it to pieces. I guess she was after the cork innards, or so it would appear, because she didn't seem too interested in the cloth covering."

"I see. Yes, naturally. But how did she go about knocking the pith helmet off your head?"

"She dropped onto it...from the ceiling."

"Sounds to me as if she lives in that ceiling."

"Maybe so. But in any case, she certainly has access to it."

"And how did you happen to go to the cellar that time? Did she lure you as before...or was this the same time?"

"No. I had gone there to lay out some traps and I guess she either heard me coming or was just at the right place at the right time."

"I see."

"And she damn near had me, too. She got herself tangled up in my feet and the only way I could escape in the end was to fall backward, out of the room, and run as fast as I could up the stairs, and she followed me all the way. I just did manage to get to the kitchen and the door closed in time. And, would you believe it, she started to gnaw on the door, trying to get at me even then?"

"That *is* somewhat hard to believe, as you suggest. But have there been other encounters you would like to tell me about?"

An inexplicable calm had come over Bart. Dr. Bissett seemed to understand, as he said, to be on Bart's side, to want to help. The more Bart talked, the more he wanted to talk, to get everything off his chest, once for all. Keeping it bottled up inside these past few days had added immeasurably to the ordeal, Bart realized now.

"Oh, yes," Bart answered. "That time that she attacked me in my bed, well, she also chewed my toothbrush to pieces and got into the toothpaste tube, not to mention a whole lot of other stuff that's been wrecked by her. But those weren't encounters in the same sense. They were more like after-the-fact provocations. The same as the other day when she got into my bedroom...while I was at work...and shit all over the bed."

"She defecated all over your bed? Is that what you're telling me?"

"Yes. Exactly. And it surely got my territorial imperative exercised, I'll tell you that, too. Makes me mad all over again, just thinking about it."

"I can imagine. Are both your parents living, Bart?"

The question took Bart by surprise. He didn't know quite what to make of it, how it tied into the problem under discussion, but he decided to play along.

"My father's been dead a number of years."

"But your mother is alive and well, presumably?"

"Yes."

"Uh...was she...would you say that she was a...a particularly domineering...or shall we say, restrictive ...parent?"

"No. Not particularly. She made it damn clear where the lines were, though."

"Yes. I see. And have you any brothers or sisters?"

"No. I'm an only child. My father used to say he was more interested in quality than in quantity." Bart laughed.

"Yes. I see. Of course. That's very amusing," Dr. Bissett said, unamused. "And, what about your wife?"

"What about my wife?"

"Would you...uh...describe her as an especially demanding person...opinionated...you know, insistent on always having her own way?"

"No. Not especially. But, like most women, she knows where her interests lie and how to defend them."

"Like *most* women?"

"Dr. Bissett...would you mind telling me just what this has to do with...?"

"It's all part of your medical profile, Bart. Routine, but necessary. Anyway, that completes those tiresome details. Now," he said, turning to a fresh sheet, "where were we?"

"I believe we were discussing the rat." Bart's tone conveyed his disapproval.

"Yes, of course," Dr. Bissett agreed with that hollow little laugh, perusing the voluminous notes he had collected. "Uh...ah, yes, here's what I'm looking for. Has anyone seen this rat...I mean, other than you, of course?"

"What's *that* supposed to mean?" Bart bridled.

"Absolutely nothing, Bart. There's nothing sinister about the question, nor any reason to get riled up over it. But, if it bothers you, there's no need to answer it."

"No. No. That's all right," Bart said contritely, feeling he might indeed have overreacted. "Come to think of it, no. No one has seen her but me. My family's been away all summer and I've been living in the house alone."

"Yes. I see."

There was a long pause while neither of them spoke. Dr. Bissett studied his notes. Bart was sitting upright on the examining table, his feet dangling over the side. He could not remember when he had changed from lying on his back.

"To go back for a minute, Bart. It's not quite clear to me from what you said. The trap. You said it was the trap that smashed your fingers. Is that correct?"

"Yes. Yes, it is."

"And how did that happen, exactly?"

"Well, I was planning to put the trap along the back wall, but as I was passing the dollhouse, it suddenly occurred to me to put it in there instead."

"I see. 'In' as inside?"

"Yes, that's right."

"And what exactly gave you that idea?'"

"Well, I was getting tired and my hand was shaking pretty badly and I didn't want this thing to go off in my hand, you know?"

"Yes, of course. That makes sense."

"Also, I wasn't having any luck the other places I was putting the traps."

"I see. And had you thought of the dollhouse before?"

"How do you mean?"

"I mean as regards the rat."

"Well, yes, as a matter of fact. Come to think of it, when I first started using the poison, I left a little pile at the front door."

"Since you had your house, it was reasonable to assume she would have hers, too. Was that your thought?"

"Yes," Bart said, preferring this lie to admitting he had done it as a joke.

"I see. So, when you decided to put the trap there, too, what happened then?"

"Well, I started to lower myself, holding the trap with one hand and reaching for the back panel with the other."

"And?"

"And, just as I started to raise the panel, she bolted out the front door on the other side."

"So, you were right, after all."

"About what?"

"In thinking that's where she made her home."

"Yes," Bart said hesitantly, deciding to play out the hand. "I suppose you could say that, yes."

"So, then what happened?"

"Well, it scared the daylights out of me and..."

"I should think so."

"And it sort of knocked me backwards, off balance, and that's when I lost control of the trap."

"And that's when it caught your fingers?"

"Exactly. Christ, it hurt! I know now how a rat must feel. And I guess I sort of blacked out."

"For how long?"

"I don't know. I just came to sitting on the floor and this goddam trap clamped onto my fingers."

"And did the rat take advantage of her good fortune?"

"You mean by attacking me?"

"Yes."

"No. I was worried sick she would, of course..."

"Naturally, you would. But she didn't?"

"No. She just hid under the furnace squealing with delight...seeing all the pain I was in."

"You couldn't see her?"

"No."

"I see. But you could hear her."

"That's right."

"And she was squealing with delight, you say?"

"That's right."

"How do you tell exactly when a rat is squealing with delight as contrasted to any other kind of squealing? Let me put that another way, Bart. How were you able to tell that her squealing was one of delight?"

"It was the same as the night she came after my...uh... up in my bed. I told you about that."

"Yes, of course. I should have thought," Dr. Bissett said, perusing his notes once more. "Let me see here. I guess that just about covers all the questions I have, Bart. I appreciate your candor." He put the yellow pad aside.

"I appreciate your interest."

"But I must ask you, where exactly do you go from here with the rat?"

"I've lost."

"I don't follow you."

"She's beaten me...or to put that the other way around, I can't beat her."

Dr. Bissett retrieved the yellow pad and started to write.

"And what does that mean, precisely?"

"I'm selling the house."

"You're *what?*"

"I can't live there with her...and she won't get out...so, I have no choice."

"Are you sure that's wise?"

"Do you have a better alternative?"

"Have you discussed this with your wife?"

"No."

"Don't you think you should?"

"She's not the one with the problem."

"Do you have a buyer...someone who's interested?"

"People coming tomorrow, as a matter of fact, and I understand they are very interested."

"But doesn't that strike you as somewhat extreme... rather like using a cannon to kill a mosquito?"

"The rat may sound like a mosquito to you, Dr. Bissett, but she's no mosquito to me."

"Forgive me, Bart...I didn't mean to denigrate..."

"It's all right, Dr. Bissett. Why the hell *should* you understand? No one else seems to, either. You're in good company."

"I wish there was something I could say to dissuade you from..."

"There's nothing. My mind is made up. It's either that or being very badly hurt by her or being driven into the booby hatch by the sheer fear of it."

"These people you say are coming to look at the house tomorrow. How do you plan to handle them?"

"From what point of view?"

"From the point of view of telling them the reason for your wanting to sell the house, of course."

Bart shrugged his shoulders.

"You will tell them the truth beforehand...about the rat. Won't you?"

"Not if I can help it."

"But the real estate agent...he knows, doesn't he?"

"Absolutely not! Christ! If I told him, or they found out in some way, all bets would be off. I mean, who the hell would go out and buy a house, knowing there's a goddam rat loose on the inside?"

"That's something of what I had in mind, Bart."

"I've got a house to sell...a rat to get rid of."

"But doesn't that strike you as somewhat reckless...not to say, unprincipled...to expose innocent people to such a hazard without even warning them, in the first place...and...and then actively luring them into buying a house you know has a fundamental flaw in it, in the second?"

"That can't be helped, Dr. Bissett."

"Perhaps not. Perhaps you're right. Well, Bart"— Dr. Bissett changed direction abruptly—"I have other patients I must see, alas. But our little talk has been most productive and informative. I hope you have found it reasonably helpful as well yourself."

"Yes, I have. I'm only sorry to have monopolized so much of your time."

"Not at all. It's what I'm here for."

"And I appreciate your listening, trying to understand, at least. That's a lot more than most people seem willing to do and it's helped me so much, just being able to talk with someone in this way. I've been so alone."

"Yes. it sounds it."

"And, please, don't think too badly of me...you know...about my not telling these people. I really am at the end of my rope."

"I can sense that."

"Just desperate."

"Well, maybe when the time comes, you'll experience a change of heart...or better yet, decide to put off selling, at least for a little while. That would still be my advice to you...for now, anyway. But we'll be seeing more of each other in the days ahead, Bart, rest assured."

They shook hands rather formally, as Bart opened the door with the frosted glass. Immediately, every eye in the waiting room focused on him. Their resentment at being kept waiting through Bart's long appointment was plain to see. He picked his way through the tangle of feet on the floor, hoping to God he wouldn't recognize anyone.

When he reached the outer door, he turned, thinking it would be courteous to wave an additional goodbye and thanks. But Dr. Bissett was already engaged in earnest conversation with the nurse at the reception desk. Bart could not hear what they were saying, of course, but he was almost certain he could make out the good doctor's lips forming the name "Eliot Riverton." The nurse nodded, picked up the telephone and started to dial.

Dr. Bissett returned to the examining room alone and shut the door.

Fifteen

Bart could not reconcile the conflicting emotions which grew out of his conference with Dr. Bissett, neither on the elevator ride back to his office, nor during the slow afternoon that ensued.

On the one hand, he thought the doctor had been kind, compassionate, genuinely concerned about him and his problem, and ready to help within the limits of his capabilities. On the other, he felt he had been scheming and deceitful, a demon making capital of Bart's obviously vulnerable condition.

Similarly, in one way, he was glad he had leveled with him to the extent that he had. It had been a relief to share this consuming burden with someone who seemed willing to listen and to learn, and not merely to question or to lecture. Yet, in another, he regretted it, feeling he had been hoodwinked into revealing too much, and that in so doing, he might have unwittingly played into Dr. Bissett's hands, and in turn Eliot Riverton's, on whatever nefarious point they were in league to prove.

But Bart and Dr. Bissett were in agreement on one thing. Phil Lavin and his clients must not be recklessly endangered. However, Bart could not go along with the idea of cancelling the visit, either directly, or indirectly through a forewarning. How to guarantee the one without jeopardizing the other thus became his number-one priority.

Bart did not think that the rat would go out of her way to attack strangers. Her grievance was with him, after all, not with them. Nor did he think that she would disclose her whereabouts, should she happen to be upstairs in the house at the time of their visit, unless provoked into it. The major open question, as Bart saw it, harrowed down to how she would interpret, and as a consequence respond to, the invasion of her personal domain.

Bart had his answer. It would be a delicate and very difficult sale, but there was no choice. He put a telephone call through to Phil Lavin.

"Phil? Is that you?" Bart inquired cheerily.

"Who's calling him?" Phil retorted, a trace of hostility in his tone. Being on the defensive came as naturally to him as the breath of life.

"Now, is that any way for a poor working slob like you to be greeting one of those rich guys like me?" Bart tweaked him with a chuckle, wanting to cast his call in as casual a light as possible.

"Uh-oh! Here it comes. I knew it. The big call off."

"On the contrary. I'm calling to confirm, actually."

"That's a relief. I'm always suspicious of you guys that can have these all-of-a-sudden changes of mind."

"Oh?" Bart reacted, unintentionally defensive himself, hoping he didn't sound it.

Phil was one of those people with an uncanny ability to smell out a situation. This sometimes led to his giving the impression that he could see more than he did.

"Yeah. They're the first to change their minds just as fast the other way."

"Oh," Bart said, relieved. "No. On the contrary. More enthusiastic than ever."

"I talked to my people, too...and they are hot to trot...I mean HOT! Be only the missus coming, though."

"Oh?" Bart saw this as possibly a bad sign.

"Not to worry. My guess is she's the one with the dough and the one that'll be making the real decisions anyhow."

"Great! As you've always been the first to admit, Phil, you're the greatest."

"You know it, baby." Phil laughed. "By the way, I meant to mention it the other day, but there's no need of you being there, you know...I mean, if you've got something more important. I know my way around the place pretty well and you can leave the key over the door or under the mat...just tell me where."

"Thanks, Phil. But to tell the truth, I'd like to be there...if that doesn't cramp your style too much, I mean." Bart wanted to sound as though he were giving Phil a choice in the matter, but in fact he had no intention of it. "I think I should, really. More polite. You know. Questions come up...I'm right there to answer them...that kind of thing."

"Hey! Not to worry. No need to sell me, pal. It's always better when the owner can be there. Makes it all look more official somehow."

"Good! That's settled, then. But I will leave the key over the door under the stoop, just in case I get tied up at the last minute and can't make it, okay?" Bart said, pleased that this first hurdle had been cleared so easily.

"Great!"

"Uh...there's one other thing, Phil. Small point, but

I've sort of been running the visit through my head a little bit...you know, trying to come up with the best scenario?"

"Yeah. Right. And I'm nuts about that fancy word, too."

"Glad you appreciate it I chose it with you in mind especially, old buddy. But seriously, I think it would be a mistake for us to show them the basement."

"Oh? How come?"

"Nothing earth-shaking," Bart answered casually. "It's just that the place is in such a goddam mess. It sort of reflects badly on the whole house, you know? I was hoping to get down there to do something about it, but there just isn't the time...unfortunately."

"Well, I sure as hell disagree with you there. I don't give a damn how much of a mess it's in. Be worse *not* to let her see it. Makes it look like you're trying to hide something."

"Maybe, but..."

"You're not, are you?"

"What's that?"

"Hiding something down there?" Phil laughed, but it was too close to home for Bart to feel much like joining in. "I mean, like some little cutie you'd just as soon not have Meg find out about?" He laughed again.

"Oh, no. Nothing like that. I wish I were." Bart forced a chuckle, thinking it might look suspect if he didn't. "It's the mess I'm thinking of."

"Hell! That doesn't matter a damn. She'll understand. These people are serious buyers, Bart, coming to look at a house, and you can't be showing it like that...piecemeal... here, you can take a look at this, but no, you can't take a look at that. It won't wash."

"That may be, Phil, but I feel very strongly on this point. I really do."

"Well, so do I, goddammit, Bart! You can't go asking me to sell your house flying on one wing. Be a waste of my time to try."

"Who said anything about selling? According to you, all you wanted to do was to show the place...and that's all I agreed to...remember?" Bart bluffed, hoping to throw him off balance, onto the defensive.

"Aw, come on, Bart. You know what I'm saying. Have a heart. It makes me look like some kind of chump, getting this babe all excited about the house and then saying to her, 'Oh, by the way, remember that playroom I was telling you is so great and you liked the idea of so much? Well, sorry about that. You can't see it.' Put yourself in her shoes."

"That's exactly where I am, Phil, believe me."

"Well, it sure doesn't sound it from the way you're talking."

Neither said anything for a few minutes, each locked in his own thoughts. Phil was the one to break the impasse.

"Jesus, Bart! If that's the way you want it, okay, to hell with it. We might as well forget the whole thing. No point even in trying."

"Okay, Phil. I hear what you're saying. Tell you what, I'll compromise with you."

"Now, you're talking."

"Beware of Greeks bearing gifts, as the man said. You haven't heard my proposition yet," Bart said disarmingly with a reassuring laugh, as if such a precaution were the last thing Phil need concern himself with.

"Okay. Good advice. And I'll take it. But stick it to me nice and easy now," Phil went along, with a laugh of his own.

"Tell you what. Since you've evidently made a big deal

about the playroom, we'll show her that. In that way, she won't be disappointed and you won't be made to feel like a chump. Okay?"

"So far, so good. But where's the kicker?"

"No kicker, Phil...and no cellar. Just the playroom. Do we have a deal?"

"No kicker, you say? Christ! That's no compromise."

"Why? All that's in there is the heating stuff, and seen one, seen 'em all, I say. And talk about filthy!"

"It'll never fly. Believe me. Never. I mean, look at yourself. Would you be caught dead buying a house without having taken a look at how the goddam place is heated, what shape it's in or nothing? Come on, Bart. Be serious."

"I am, Phil, and I'm afraid it's the best I can come up with, in the circumstances."

"What circumstances? What circumstances could make you come up with such a damn-fool idea? There *is* something down there you're not telling me about. Got to be. I mean, I'm just kidding, of course...but you've got to be putting me on, too...I hope?"

"Trust me, Phil. I'm as anxious to get these people to buy this house as you are, believe me...more, even," Bart said solemnly. "And I know exactly what I'm doing."

"Yeah, well, maybe. Okay. Have it your way...*for now*," Phil agreed reluctantly, pausing to let the last two words convey his full meaning, "but it sure beats the living hell out of me what you're up to over there, I'll tell you that."

Phil was right, needless to say, and he had every reason to be as annoyed as he was with Bart. Anyone could recognize it as an unworkable compromise on its face, and the truce that it brought was an uneasy one at best. But it was also, both realized, the most either of them could hope for and it would, therefore, have to suffice, at any rate as Phil had stressed so pointedly, "for now."

Bart left the office around four, partially to combat his restiveness, but mostly to give himself an extra hour at home that evening in which to straighten out the house and to ready it for inspection the following day. It was a sound decision.

With his arm still in a sling, everything took him twice as long as it should have and required at least that much more in added output. When he had finished, however, the house was much improved and showed not a sign of the life-and-death struggle that had been raging for so long within its walls. Only the playroom remained to be done, but this would have to wait. It was late, Bart was wrung dry and, with his arm impaired, it was plainly too risky to tackle any part of the basement at that point.

And so, he hastened up to bed instead, hoping to cram in as much sleep as he could before the rat warmed to her nocturnal harassment. That part of the night ended for him four hours later and the remainder was a question of just holding on until the light of day and it was time to leave for the office.

With each passing hour Friday morning, Bart's cold feet grew more severe. Phil's parting salvo of "for now" pounded in his head with the force and persistence of a pneumatic hammer. He was every bit as headstrong as Bart, and with him so intent on circumventing Bart's caveat on the cellar, there was no telling where all that could lead.

Several times Bart put calls through to him both at his home and at his office. But it was as though Phil could sense what was in the wind and made sure to be at neither number. Finally, it had been too late and the decision to go ahead had made itself. Bart would have to make the best of it, and at bottom, this was doubtless what he wanted.

He counted on needing roughly an hour to make the playroom presentable and left the office accordingly. But taxis were scarce and traffic crawled uptown on both Park and Third Avenue. It was one of those rare instances when the subway would have been preferable, but once committed to his choice, he was stuck with it. The hour he had hoped for was cut to half that

Bart wanted to change into his battle gear, but with so much to do in the playroom, there might not be enough time left to get out of them before Phil and his client arrived at the front door. Not only would he look like a jackass greeting them dressed like a lumberjack, but also, and more serious, it would give his plot away. No, it was a calculated risk he would simply have to take.

He removed the sling, tested his arm, his hand, and was pleased to find both functional. Better yet, his fingers were free of the throbbing that had afflicted them whenever he had removed the sling before. He tossed it onto the island counter, took off his suit jacket, his tie, rolled up his shirt sleeves, and was ready to go to work.

Bart glanced at his watch, reconsidered the decision about the hunting clothes, decided to stick to it. He took two deep breaths and then a third, clutched the fireplace poker hard, wrenched open the door and bounded down the playroom stairs.

At the bottom, he quickly sized up the problem. Not as large as he had imagined. But the cellar door was open and the light burning inside. Carefully, he edged toward the opening, his back glued to the wall. When he thought he was within reach, he stretched for it and yanked the door shut, snapping the string that had been holding it.

He slumped against the wall gratefully, panting, as much from nerves as from exertion. So far, so good.

Gradually he regained both his composure and his wind. He leaned the fireplace poker against the wall and wasted no more time before getting down to the work at hand. Within a surprisingly short span, the place began to look less like a disaster area and more like a playroom..."

Throughout, Bart kept a sharp vigil for the rat, always aware that she might jump out at him at any moment. But she didn't, and when he had finished the job, he was certain she was nowhere in the room. This meant she was either locked in the cellar or was somewhere in the upper reaches of the house. In either case, she was relatively neutralized, but that was all the more reason for Bart to control the visit throughout and to make absolutely sure Phil Lavin and his client stayed on this side of the barn-red fire door.

Bart checked his watch. Ten minutes to go. He could have donned his battle gear after all. But it was of no consequence. He had gambled and won. Besides, he could use the time left for a quick run through the house to correct any last-minute details.

Standing at the foot of the stairs, hands on his hips, he surveyed his work. The decision to let Phil show the playroom had been a good one. It looked great. Bart smiled with satisfaction.

The rat sprang at him, landing squarely in the middle of his back, digging her claws into him, consolidating her perch. She had been hiding on one of the playroom stairs.

"Oh-h-h-h, God!" Bart cried out, wriggling his back, contorting, desperately trying to get her off him, running around the room, flapping his arms wildly. The rat dug her claws in deeper, shredding his shirt.

"Oh-h-h-h, God!" he wailed again, throwing himself

to the floor, on his back. Her corpulent body compressed itself against his, her claws penetrated his flesh deeper still. He rolled over and over around the floor, again and again, trying to crush her with his own weight, to no avail.

Bart jumped back up on his feet, hopped up and down, twisted, contorted some more, reached over his shoulders for her with both hands, poking at her, hoping to knock her off balance and off him, coming so close he could feel her whiskers brush his bare fingers, even her hot breath. She was squealing merrily now.

"Oh, God, oh, God!" he pleaded, starting to run wildly about the room once more, somehow to relieve the pain she was inflicting. Was she gnawing into him, too?

His back felt as though someone were holding ten thousand lighted cigarettes against it. Deeper and deeper the claws did their work, ripping his flesh, gouging, torturing.

Bart spotted the sharp edge of the stairwell wall, ran to it and started brushing his back past it. Maybe this would succeed in knocking her off. Closer and closer he came to the wall, but each time she managed to compress her mushy body as she had before, finding refuge even in the slight depression between his shoulder blades. Closer and closer he moved. Flatter and flatter she flattened herself.

Finally, convinced he was about to go stark raving mad if he didn't get her off him, he moved still closer, planted his feet firmly on the floor and gave his torso a violent, wrenching twist.

The rat let out a blood-curdling squeal. Bart saw stars, felt as though he had just been hit with a sledgehammer. He was about to pass out, fought to prevent it, thought he might have broken his back.

The rat had been knocked to the floor and was racing for cover at the other end of the room. Bart was in such a state of shock and pain that he didn't notice her falling, only managing to glimpse her scooting under a pile of toys at the far end of the room, one of those he had just finished stacking so neatly.

He desperately wanted to sit down, to rest, to close his eyes, recuperate, but forced himself to go after her, kicking insanely into the pile, sending toys flying everywhere and her scurrying for cover elsewhere.

Bart bounded after her, kicking wildly into her new sanctuary. Pain smashed into his shin bone, but he didn't care. He was as though crazed, no longer able to feel more or to think beyond his single-minded determination to flush her into the open where he could destroy her once for all. Again, he kicked into the stack, sending more toys through the air.

He looked for the fireplace poker, couldn't remember where he had put it, settled on a child's baseball bat instead.

"Come out of there, goddam you!" he bellowed at her, glowering down at the spot where he thought she was. "I know you're in there." He delivered another fearsome kick.

And there she was, in the open, toys all around her but not one to hide under.

Bart saw that she was huffing and puffing as badly as he, her sides expanding and contracting furiously.

She was curled into a ball, looking up at him, cringing, expectant.

Bart was seized by a sudden pity for her. She was so small, helpless, clearly incapable of further resistance. He suffered an acute pang of conscience about killing her, forgetting momentarily all that she had done to him.

Her eyes flickered between him and the bat he held, menacingly waving over her head.

He wished there could be another way, but knew there wasn't. He debated how best to deliver the death blow. It must be swift, sure, merciful. Certainly, she had earned no less.

She let out a small squeal, terrified, pleading. He hesitated. She had won the delay she needed.

Instantly she took off, scampering up the wall as though she had been a fly, reaching the acoustical tile ceiling within a split second.

Bart took a fierce swipe at her with the baseball bat, missed, tearing a large hole in the ceiling instead. He swung again. Again, she just managed to dodge clear. Then, she jumped, aiming straight for his exposed face and neck. He twisted, ducked, whimpered. She brushed his bare cheek. Instinctively he put his hand to it, drew it away. It was smeared with blood from where she had mutilated him either with her teeth or her outstretched claws. Blood trickled down his face onto his sweaty shirt front.

Again, Bart was in hot pursuit kicking, flailing, kicking. Once more he had her in the open.

She tried to scamper away. Bart's foot shot out, catching her by the tail. Her feet spun, she squirmed, contorted, strained like a dog on a leash but he held her there.

The doorbell rang.

Deliberately, almost ceremoniously, Bart raised the bat high and plunged the tip home with full fury. The rat's entire body lifted, went rigid, as though administered an electric charge, quivered and then fell limp.

"That's funny!" Phil Lavin mused, pushing the doorbell again, harder. "He said he'd be here. Oh, well..." he said, feigning disappointment and reaching for the key Bart had said he would leave over the doorframe. "We might as well

go on in anyhow—give us a chance to look at the cellar while we're waiting for him," Phil said with a satisfied glint in *his eye.*

Bart slumped against the playroom wall and slowly slid down to the floor.

A pool of blood formed around the rat's crushed head like a swelling halo.

Phil Lavin waved to Dr. Bissett and Eliot Riverton as their taxicab drew up in front of the house. He had been waiting for them on the stoop, not knowing how to cope with Bart on his own. He introduced himself and started to run once more through the tale of horror he had recounted over the telephone, leading the way hurriedly downstairs as he did so.

"Jesus, God!" Eliot Riverton gasped at what he saw, feeling suddenly faint, groping for the handrail to steady himself.

Bart was lying on his side on the playroom floor, his eyes glazed, his jaw slack, his face the color and texture of marble, except for where the rat had slashed open his left cheek. His shirt was in tatters drenched in sweat and blood. He was shaking feverishly and whimpering softly.

The rat, only a few feet away, lay still and stiff in her own darkening pool of blood.

Eliot and Phil watched silently from the sidelines as Dr. Bissett ministered to Bart, readying him for the trip to the hospital. Their expressions of alarm and morbid fascination mirrored each other.

EPILOGUE

FOUR WEEKS to the day after his ordeal had begun, Bart was well enough to travel and Meg took him with her to Maine for the balance of the month. While they were away, she saw to the thorough cleaning of the house and to the removal of all vestige of what had transpired there, so that by the family's return after Labor Day, it was sparkling once more, a real home to come back to.

But it was no good. The house held too many memories, too many reminders, real or imagined. It had been violated beyond redemption.

Bart priced it to sell and it did so quickly, the ecstatic new owner taking possession in early November, still shaking his head wondrously at having found "so much house" for "such a bargain."

Coincidentally, Bart and Meg were able to move the family into their new home the same day. It was a good piece of luck.

When they had first been told about it, their immediate reaction had been to reject it out of hand. With such a fashionable address and convenient location, it was bound to be beyond their financial reach, but the real estate broker whose listing it was had persuaded them to "just take a look."

It was a ten-room apartment on the eighth floor of a modern, clean, well-maintained co-op just east of Park Avenue. They fell in love with it at first sight and winked knowingly at each other when hearing the price. Bart, being a good businessman, put in a bid suitably lower and, to his delight, it was accepted.

Settling in after a long day of moving, Bart stood on the top rung of a small aluminum ladder, cleaning kitchen cupboards too high for Meg to reach comfortably. The girls were gleefully running all about the apartment, exploring every nook and cranny, exulting over every discovery. Little Bart tried valiantly to keep up with them, dragging his portable playpen over the freshly polished floors. Meg was putting away the china and glassware. Neither she nor Bart had spoken in some time, too involved in their work, too tired, or both.

Suddenly, she broke their silence. "Bart?" There was an unmistakable note of apprehension in her voice.

"What's the problem, sweetheart?" Bart answered gently, catching it.

"Bart...what are these? I keep running into them."

"What's that?" he asked, descending from his perch and going toward her.

"These," she said, pointing into the drawer.

The drawer she had just opened was littered with small pellets. They were dark brown, almost black, and shaped more or less like grains of rice, although of a different texture and slightly larger...

www.ingramcontent.com/pod-product-compliance
Lightning Source LLC
Chambersburg PA
CBHW010346220726
48290CB00016B/2656